JEZEBEL, WILLIE
AND THE VOICE

AN AMERICAN POLITICAL FABLE

JOHN L. HARMER

Published by
Legends Library Publishing, Inc.
Rochester, NY

www.legendslibrary.org
info@legendslibrary.com
877-222-1960

ISBN: 978-1-944200-19-0

Printed in the United States of America

Cover designed by Alisha Bishop

Interior designed by Jacob F. Frandsen

AUTHOR'S NOTE

In 1992, when Arkansas Governor William J. Clinton became the nominee for President for the Democratic Party, I began keeping a file of press clippings and media reports regarding the various Clinton scandals. During that twenty-four year period I have also purchased and read many of the books that have been authored by highly credible individuals in which the Clinton's contempt for truth, integrity, dignity, and principle have been well documented. Some of these books and many of these articles from the press are cited in the bibliography at the end of this book.

When it became apparent in March of 2016 that Hillary Clinton would be the Democratic nominee for president, I decided to find a way to summarize the materials contained in those files. It soon became obvious that it would take nearly a thousand pages to do justice to that effort. It was also obvious that very few people would be willing to take the time to read the entire account of the Bill Clinton's voracious obsession with sex and Hillary's overwhelming lust for money. The only way that I could make it possible to reveal the total lack of dignity, integrity, and principle in these two people was to create a fable about two imaginary people named Jezebel and Willie.

The dictionary definition of the word "fable" is "a fictitious narrative or statement; . . . a narration intended to enforce a useful truth . . . to write or talk about as if true" (*Webster's Collegiate Dictionary,* 7th ed.).

Thus this book about Bill and Hillary Clinton has been written based upon actual events that have been widely reported in the printed and electronic media. Those events are presented here in the format of a fictionalized fable only because of the logistical challenge of documenting them and their actuality in the lives of the Clintons.

The only principal character is the book who does not in fact represent an actual participant in the events recited in the book is the individual referred to as the Voice. In my more than fifty years of active participation in the political world of Washington, D.C., I encountered this individual on many occasions. He actually exists. He actually frequented the While House during the Clinton era. By the skillful use of the hundreds of millions of dollars at his disposal, he stopped congressional investigations, congressional committee hearings, and appellate court reviews of lower court decisions. He secured the appointment of his many subservient puppets to senior positions in the government. Other than the Clintons, he was the most evil person that I ever encountered.

After careful study of the death of former Clinton associate Vincent Foster, I am personally convinced that he was murdered. In this book, I have been careful not to ascribe to the Clinton's the responsibility for his murder. At the same time, the absolute refusal of the Clintons to allow access to Vincent Foster's files after his death is nothing less than the obstruction of justice on their part, for which they should have been held accountable.

John L. Harmer, Esq.
8 July 2016

PROLOGUE

Kathy Christiansen lived and worked as a journalist in the largest state of the federal union. She was an editor as well as a commentator at the *Capitol Times*, the state capitol's daily newspaper. She was widely recognized for her ability to present complicated issues of public concern in an accurate and understandable chronology. She was also respected for her integrity as a journalist as well as for her insightful analysis of current issues as a columnist in the editorial department for the largest newspaper in the state.

She had followed with an initial suspicion of danger which was ultimately confirmed as a reality the emergence and ultimate success of an attorney politician named Willie Hilton and his wife, Jezebel. From his remarkable upset victory four years earlier in the race for the office of Attorney General she had agonized at how Willie and Jezebel had been able to obfuscate the facts involved with the repeated scandals that surrounded their personal and political lives. Now in the face of his imminent election to the office of governor, the mission which had thundered inside her head for four years had to be fulfilled.

With the election for the office of Governor only ten days away she had come to her office early on a Saturday morning to write what she knew would be her final editorial commentary on the lives of Willie and Jezebel. She knew that the same unknown force that had been present from the beginning of their political careers would make certain that what she was about to write would never be published by the *Times*.

In Kathy's daily journals she had faithfully recorded the numerous instances of criminal conduct in the lives of Jezebel and Willie during the prior four years. However, the ultimate political obscenity had recently been achieved by the Hiltons with the creation of a charitable foundation dedicated to helping children all over the world who were the innocent victims of disease, natural disasters, and political turmoil. In fact the foundation's primary purpose was to enable individuals, foreigners, and criminal entities who otherwise could not legally make donations to the Hilton's political careers could now do so without being circumscribed by the laws surrounding contributions to political campaigns.

It is ironic that two of the women in the Capitol who kept meticulous daily journals had such different motives. "Sweet Tammy Hinsey" as she was known among the rock and roll fraternity, wanted to be sure that she had "perfected her technique" (to use her own words) as she pursued her promiscuous sexual life. Later in Willie's political career her journal entry regarding Willie Hilton would be discovered by a writer doing research for an article for *Penthouse* magazine.

Kathy Christiansen also kept a meticulous daily journal. She recorded the names of people that she would interview as she pursued her career as a serious journalist. Since those names were often people of note she would usually enter a descriptive comment about how she felt after the interview.

This fall Saturday morning Kathy was alone in the editorial offices of the *Capitol Times*. The employees who would produce the final sections of the Sunday edition were two floors below her. Kathy savored the serenity of the solitude as she continued to search through the several volumes of her journals that were opened on her desk. The fall air outside was cool but the sky was clear. "Ideal football weather," she thought as she turned once again to her computer in order to compose another paragraph.

Also on her desk was a letter from the publisher of one of the nation's most respected publications inviting her to come to New York to be interviewed for the position of Associate Editor. Kathy had struggled with the conflicting emotions that prevented her from making a decision about the offer. She loved her job, she was respected and often adulated by important people in the Capitol. Though she was considered a very attractive woman there had never been a romantic interlude that might result in marriage.

However, her mission this morning was not the letter from New York. Willie Hilton had announced in the spring that he would run for Governor. He had easily won the primary election with an early media campaign of such magnitude and sophistry that his competitors had no chance to overtake him.

Now it was the next to last weekend before the November general election. Several weeks earlier Kathy had decided that it was time for someone, meaning herself, to take a closer look at the wife of the man who would likely be the next Governor of the State. Her search through her journal for the prior four years was to refresh her memory of times when Jezebel was visibly involved in the affairs of State.

INTRODUCTION

Jezebel and Willie met in law school. She was ambitious, disciplined and extremely skillful in manipulating other people. He was handsome, reckless, intelligent, articulate, persuasive of others, and obsessed with sex. He was a perfect fit for an ambitious woman looking for a puppet who could give her the credibility she needed in a male dominated culture. When their first date ended up with an all-night stand in her apartment, she knew that she had found her man.

They became active in the campus student Democratic club. He could schmooze an individual, a small group, or a large audience of political partisans. She was the exact opposite. She hated to do all of the public things at which he was so good. Together theirs was a marriage made in hell.

In their senior year of law school they were active volunteers in a local campaign for the State Senate. So intense did their involvement become that the dean of the law School had to call them to his office and with a stern warning made it clear that they were in danger of being flunked out of law school even in their senior year.

Willie had a distant cousin named John Vincent who was also in their class. John Vincent was also very intelligent, very disciplined, and very determined to graduate at the top of the class. In their senior year he was the Editor of the Law Review and would certainly be the acknowledged winner of the coveted "Order of the Coif" honor for the outstanding senior student.

John Vincent did not share their interest in politics. However, as soon as they had met she recognized how valuable he could be and throughout the time from their marriage until graduation she entwined him into their social circle. She made certain that Willie and his cousin were "best friends."

When the November election was over and their candidate had won the State Senate seat they recruited Cousin John as a tutor for both of them. With his help they passed their exams and entered their last semester of law school confident that they had found their destiny. Willie would ultimately become the candidate and she the campaign manager. Her ambition and his effervescent personality would ultimately make it possible for them to have that for which they both lusted, money, power, and fame.

Here was their story as Kathy had watched it unfold over the past four years.

1

THE FIRST CAMPAIGN

Willie was standing at the desk of the Secretary to the President of the Springville Foundation, the largest and most respected charity in the state. The foundation was endowed by the President's great grandfather who had made a fortune in the oil and gas industry. The Foundation took its name from the small town where the President's great grandfather had drilled his first oil well. The Great Grandfather's financial endowment allowed the Foundation to support the arts and the many local causes for the benefit of the poor and the needy. It also gave the foundation a huge legacy of good will and prestige. The large endowment allowed his son and grandson to carry on with his generosity.

Shortly after opening their law office Jezebel and Willie had volunteered to assist the Armstrong House, one of the small local charities that each year received a generous check from the Springville foundation. The primary mission of the Armstrong House was to provide help for abandoned children. The skill of Jezebel in enhancing the effectiveness of the charity's management soon came to the attention of the CEO of the Springville Foundation. The CEO had invited Willie to come to his office for an interview but had inadvertently omitted Jezebel from the invitation.

Their meeting was not long as the CEO came right to the point. "We have watched what you have been accomplishing with the folks at the Armstrong House. You have been remarkable in strengthening their management and enhancing their community support. There are several similar entities around the state that we have been helping that could use that kind of assistance in improving their operations. Would you be interested in a small retainer to work for us by coaching some of these other charities?"

Willie immediately turned on the charm. He feigned modesty at the compliments given to him by the CEO and then proceeded with a sales pitch of what he felt he and Jezebel could do for similar beneficiaries of the Springville Foundation. At the end of a twenty minute conversation there was a handshake between the two men to confirm a proposal that Willie submit an "engagement letter" to the CEO for the services of their law firm.

As Willie left the CEO must have pondered, ". . . that's interesting. He did not even ask how much the retainer would be." He then told his secretary to be on the watch for a letter to come from Willie's and Jezebel's law firm.

As soon as he was safely out of any possibility of being heard by someone from the offices of the Foundation Willie phoned Jezebel at their office. As soon as Willie had received the phone call inviting him to come to the CEO's office Jezebel had been beside herself with anxious anticipation. With trembling hands she listened to Willies' recital of the brief conversation and the request from the CEO.

"This is great!" she exclaimed. "This will give us the opportunity to get close to small charities around the state. Soon they will think that we are the Springville Foundation."

As soon as Willie was back at the office Jezebel was ready with an agenda that took them the rest of the day and late into the evening to discuss. In that discussion Willie failed to mention how attractive the CEO's secretary was. Nor did he mention the wedding ring on her left hand.

For the next year Jezebel and Willie met with the founders of a variety of small charitable entities about the state. Some of these were sponsored by churches. Others were simply the work of good citizens trying to help solve a social welfare problem in their community. Thanks to Jezebel's single-mindedness these small charities were enhanced in their ability to raise funds and to attract the support of many more people in their local community.

After graduation from law school, Willie's cousin John Vincent accepted an opportunity to join the largest and most prestigious law firm in the state. After his first year the firm moved him into the Mergers and Acquisitions (M&A) group of the firm. Even though the local office of the firm had over one hundred attorneys it was not a stand-alone entity but rather the local office in the State Capitol of a world-wide firm with head offices in New York. John Vincent's keen intellect and his self-discipline earned him many additional responsibilities in the M&A group. He quickly made rapid advancement in the firm.

Jezebel made certain that the Springville Foundation would not quibble with her retainer proposal when Willie submitted it to the CEO. She and Willie immediately began making contact with other recipients of the Springville Foundation. Within a year they had a working relationship with over half of the entities that were legally classified as "charities" to whom the Springville Foundation made an annual donation. About half of these entities were sponsored by local Churches.

Three years after opening their own law firm Jezebel and Willie were still struggling financially. As part of their work for the Springville Foundation, Willie had gone to a mid-sized city about forty miles south of the state capitol. His mission was to give a talk to some of the donors to a small local charity that was partially supported by the Springville Foundation. During the dinner with the Chairman and Board of Directors prior to the formal meeting, Willie sat across the table from an attractive woman who had no rings on her left hand. Willie made certain that during the dinner their eyes met for long enough to convey a message to the woman that Willie would like to get to know her better.

As soon as his talk was over and as he was saying goodbye to his hosts, the woman who had been sitting opposite Willie shook his hand as she said goodnight. She left in his hand a note that simply had a phone number on it. When it was an opportune moment to make the call she gave Willie the directions to her home.

Several hours later during the drive back to the Capitol his cell phone rang. When he answered it was Jezebel, who was furious. "You idiot!" she screamed. "I have been calling you for hours. How long before you can get here?"

"Sorry," replied Willie. "As always they wanted to talk and talk and talk before I was finally able to get away. What's up?"

Now Jezebel's voice was more in control. She did not care about the fact that she had just been informed by the hostess for the event that Willie had left several hours earlier. That was what she had learned to expect whenever he was off alone.

"Soon after you left this afternoon the Attorney General held an unscheduled press conference. He has made the decision not to run for re-election so that he can accept a cushy job with the Department of Justice in Washington. This is our chance. It will be an open race with no incumbent. The filing deadline is in two days. We have got to get your candidate papers filed with the Secretary of State. We are going to win that election."

Willie's adrenaline gushed to the highest possible potency. His mind raced with the realization that this would move them into the upper realms of the social network in the state capitol. At long last the dreams for which they had yearned could actually become a reality.

When he came through the door Jezebel had printed out a "time and task" calendar starting that night and running up to the primary election. He dutifully sat down at her desk as she handed him his copy of the campaign strategy. Yes, he would be the candidate but there was no reason to even discuss the obvious. She would make the decisions. She was brutally frank in making it clear to him that there would be no more toleration of his duplicitous life style. Even the hint of a scandal would destroy all of her dreams. Willie may be the horse but she would always be holding the reins. And she would hold them very tight.

It was well past mid-night when they finally decided to end the day.

The law firm that had hired John Vincent even before he had graduated was also the primary law firm for the Springville Foundation. However, John was unaware of how Jezebel and Willie had been retained by the Foundation. After three years with the firm he was still an "associate" and not a partner in the firm. His area of expertise was in the Mergers & Acquisitions section of the firm. Thus Vincent was surprised to bump into Willie and the CEO of the Springville Foundation coming out of the office of his supervising partner. Willie was quite effusive in his introduction of the CEO to John while still in the presence of the senior partner.

That night Willie had recited to Jezebel the dynamics of the surprise meeting with John Vincent. In so doing he never mentioned why he and the CEO were at the law firm.

"Why were you and the CEO at the law firm?" asked Jezebel.

"The Springville Foundation has been approached about joining a syndicate of tax exempt foundations around the U.S. and in other countries in Europe and Asia" said Willie. "The purpose is to unite in giving support to what they consider to be 'worthy' causes. The CEO knows that the law firm has a large office in New York and wanted to have someone from the firm go with him to New York for the meeting with the other foundation CEO's."

By that time Jezebel had lost interest in John Vincent's career as a lawyer.

Jezebel threw herself into Willie's campaign with the intensity that she had pursued other objectives in her life. The intention of the incumbent Attorney General with the timing of his announcement not to seek re-election was to limit as much as possible the number of candidates for the office.

When the filing period closed there were only two other candidates for the office of Attorney General. One was the incumbent's Chief Deputy who the incumbent had hand-picked to succeed him. The other was a well-known judge of the state appellate court. There would be a primary election to select the final candidate to appear on the ballot.

Jezebel immediately began an intense scrutiny of their two opponents. Meanwhile there was the necessity to create a campaign organization. Here the serendipity of representing the Springville Foundation presented the first of many unexpected gifts to Jezebel and Willie. Through their efforts with the many small charities throughout the state who were beneficiaries of the Springville Foundation they had met a large number of people who were active in their local community. Together they went through their files of these small charities and soon had a state-wide list of more than fifty names of people to contact on Willie's behalf. Most of these would be recruited to be local community chairpersons for Willie.

Critical now would be someone who could be trusted to carry out Jezebel's instructions as the de facto campaign manager. Almost simultaneously they thought of John Vincent. "He would be perfect," said Willie. "But there is no way that the law firm would let him do it." Even Willie, whose competence as a lawyer was always on shaky ground understood that someone in John Vincent's position at the firm would be putting in sixty plus hours a week. "There is no way that they would let him do it," said Willie.

"Yes there is," said Jezebel.

"Like how?" said Willie.

"Never mind for now," said Jezebel.

However, in this instance, Willie was right and Jezebel was proven wrong. She had counted on the fact that she had compensated John Vincent for his tutoring services during the last year of law school with her personal intimacy. In this instance there was an actual bond of affection between the two as well as the physical cohabiting. She had counted on that bond to persuade Vincent to take a leave of absence from the firm in order to manage the campaign.

John Vincent knew better than to even ask.

As the weeks went by Jezebel skillfully planted stories with printed and electronic media about the incumbent AG's Chief Deputy. She found the fodder for those stories through an intense study of his history. His law school was in the second or third tier of law schools in the state. Jezebel was able through a friend who was also on the faculty at the university where the Chief Deputy had graduated from law school to get a surreptitious copy of his grades. There were two "incompletes" on his grade record. Although he had later accomplished the requirements to complete the courses and obtain the passing grade Jezebel was able to ghostwrite "letters to the editor" of daily papers in the state that made it appear that the Chief Deputy had actually failed the courses.

She also found a question about his lack of military service. She was familiar with this issue because Willie had skillfully avoided his military obligation by becoming a "student" at an obscure college in northwestern Canada.

Finally she found an item in one of the daily newspapers outside the capitol city where the Chief Deputy had presented an award to a business man who several months later was indicted by a grand jury for money laundering charges.

With these and several other phony issues Jezebel was able to recruit local citizens to raise questions whenever the Chief Deputy made a public appearance. He was on the defensive before every audience and in every electronic media interview. His viability as a candidate became weaker with each new issue that she floated through their state-wide cadre of campaign supporters.

The appellate court judge was more of a problem. No matter how hard she searched she could not find anything that could be spun or twisted into an issue of questionable competence or integrity.

When the primary election was only three weeks away Willie was off campaigning in the far northwest corner of the state.

He had become a "poster child" candidate that the media had picked up and enhanced. His handsome appearance, his affable personality, his quick wit on camera and with the newspaper's editorial boards had produced a groundswell of support.

Nonetheless, notwithstanding Jezebel's skillful assassination of the Chief Deputy's character, the polls showed that Willie was still in a distant third place among the three candidates. In the midst of this intense turmoil Willie got a call from the CEO of the Foundation.

"I need you and your wife to accompany me to New York," he said. "There is a meeting of some of the CEO's in our industry. I want to have the two of you tell them about your efforts on our behalf with the smaller charities. We will pay all of the expenses. You will stay at one of the best five star hotels in New York. My secretary will call you tomorrow with all of the details."

The CEO did not even wait for an answer. He simply hung up. Willie was still in deep thought about the CEO's very attractive secretary when it did occur to him that they were in the middle of a campaign. "We can't possibly go now," he thought. "She will take my head off if I even suggest it."

Now another serendipitous gift saved Willie's head. Cousin John Vincent called shortly after the call from the CEO. "Willie," he said, "I know that you have been invited to go to New York with your CEO. It would never occur to him that you are in the middle of a campaign. I just talked with Jezebel and now I'm telling you, I don't care what other issues are involved, you absolutely have to make that trip. Let me tell you why. The two of you will meet a dozen of the most powerful men in the world. If they are impressed with you the financial struggle in your campaign will be over. Just trust me. Jezebel has already agreed to go."

They made the trip and just as John Vincent had explained, the CEO had arranged to get Jezebel and Willie a fifteen minute slot on the day-long agenda. Since Jezebel had done most of the work with the small charities and since there was only fifteen minutes allotted to them Jezebel determined that she would make the presentation alone. During the break in the agenda before Jezebel's presentation Willie's job was to circulate among the attendees, to find out who they were and where they lived.

Jezebel hated speaking to any group, but she soon realized that this group represented more money and more power than she could possibly have imagined. Jezebel summoned all of her resourcefulness in order to make certain that at the end of her fifteen minutes the attendees would certainly remember her name.

Jezebel was effective but with only fifteen minutes she did not have the ability to awaken the audience to anything more than a polite round of applause.

There was one individual in particular who had politely but emphatically made Willie to understand that he did not appreciate Willie's interrogation. Willie was sensitive enough to back away immediately. This man had listened quite attentively to Jezebel's presentation. When she was finished he briefly shook her hand and congratulated her on the success of their endeavors with the small charities.

John Vincent had also listened to Jezebel's presentation. He had instructed Jezebel to bring a supply of campaign brochures and donation envelopes on the trip to New York. In an appropriate way he was able during the next two days to have a brief conversation with most of the attendees. At the end of each conversation he was able to give the attendee with whom he was speaking a copy of the brochure along with a donation envelope. That night most of the brochures and envelopes ended up in the waste basket in each attendee's room.

When Jezebel and Willie arrived back at their home in the state Capitol they found that an independent poll conducted by the Political Science Department at one of the campus' of the State University had shown Willie to be within five percentage points of the other two candidates. Too late the incumbent's deputy realized that he would not automatically inherit his mentor's office. The false issues that Jezebel had managed to plant with the printed and electronic media had effectively put the Deputy A.G. on the defensive. Instead of running a strong positive campaign he was constantly spending time explaining away the baseless accusations that Jezebel had managed to plant against him.

Another intense week of campaigning by Willie mobilized their volunteers about the state. But now there were bills to be paid for printing and postage for which there were no funds. Willie was using several credit cards just to keep enough gas in his car to make the next campaign appointment. The election was now just a little over two weeks away. In addition to Willie's car the campaign itself was in danger of running out of "emotional "gas.

Late into the night Jezebel kept up a grueling mental review of all possible sources for some funds. They had borrowed from their bank everything that their credit could qualify for. Their volunteers were loyal but they were in no position to make meaningful financial contributions in addition to their hours of volunteer labor. Willie and Jezebel had also borrowed from all of their family members and friends on top of the donations that those friends had made.

Just past 10:00 p.m. her phone rang. They each had a phone with a special number for the campaign. Her caller ID showed no name or number. Confident at first that it was some telemarketer she ignored it. Upon reflection she decided to take the call since it was well past the legal hour for a telemarketer.

A voice that she had never heard before spoke slowly, clearly, and with an evident assurance of power. The voice simply said: "Tomorrow at 10:00 a.m. you will get a phone call from an investment broker. He will explain to you an option for some cattle futures. You will need to put up a thousand dollars for the option. Two days later you will get a call from a different party offering to buy your option for one hundred thousand dollars. Do not foul this up. Just keep your idiot husband out of the way." With that cryptic message the caller hung up.

Her first thought was that it was a scheme to trick them into a trap that would cost the election. Her second thought was that she didn't have one thousand dollars. After some further reflection she decided that it was some type of hoax.

While she was still trying to unscramble the phone call Willie came in from his last campaign event of the night. He was usually empowered by one of these events from listening to the assurances of victory that would come from the fawning political "wannabes" who were always managing to be present even though they made no contribution to the campaign. Tonight he just slumped down into a chair.

"How many people were there?" She asked.

Willie, out of habit, doubled the number of attendees up to ". . . over a hundred."

Then, with several profane expletives he simply said, ". . . we can win this thing if we can just find a hundred grand. We will never have another chance like this again. With two terms as The A.G. I can become the Governor."

Jezebel just looked at Willie and though her countenance did not reveal her contempt for him she decided to make one last effort to borrow the thousand dollars that the Voice had said she would need. Willie went for a hot shower and she phoned Willie's cousin, John Vincent.

It was nearly midnight but Vincent was still in his office at the law firm. She skillfully manipulated him by asking if he had ever heard back from any of the people they met in New York. Of course he had not but remained hopeful that soon someone would come through.

Now that she had him on the defensive she said, "Look. We are neck and neck with both of the other candidates. Willie just came back from an event that had over two hundred people in attendance. We are getting crowds like that all over the state. But we are broke. We desperately need about five thousand dollars to pay for a last minute burst of radio and TV ads. Is there any way that you could make us another loan?"

Vincent remained silent for thirty seconds which seemed like ten minutes to Jezebel. Finally he said, "I could loan you another thousand but I absolutely have to get it back."

"Great!" she replied in exuberance. "You will get it back. That's a promise." Although John Vincent was emotionally bonded to Jezebel he had now known her for over five years. In his mind her "promise" was as worthless as Willie's commitment of loyalty in the marriage. On the other hand, ". . . maybe they just might win," he thought.

They arranged for her to pick up the check first thing in the morning. Once that she had the check she immediately went to the bank and deposited it. She had now convinced herself to believe the unknown voice on the phone. It was imperative that when the investment broker phoned she had to be able to come across with a thousand dollars.

Promptly at 10:00 a.m., the phone call came. The caller did not introduce himself. He simply followed the exact script that the voice had given to Jezebel. He gave her some instructions on where to wire the thousand dollars and she gave to him the necessary instructions on where to e-mail the confirmation of the purchased option. She then started to ask about the identity of the "voice" but before she could finish the sentence the caller had hung up.

Willie had left early for a day of campaign events. The volunteers at the campaign headquarters were busy putting together a rally for Willie that evening. Jezebel had a pile of critical phone messages to answer but all that she could think about was the phone call. "Can this be real?" "Have I just been swindled out of a thousand dollars?"

Her agony made it impossible to eat and drink. But in the mid-afternoon the promised option certificate arrived via e-mail. Jezebel examined it again and again. She had to talk to someone so she called John Vincent. Without disclosing any of the details she asked him how to go about confirming an option certificate. Everything that he said had to be there was there. Her instincts served her well when she decided not to pursue the authentication issue any further.

Kathy now switched from writing in the first person to writing as a third person observer. "In the editorial offices of the *Capitol Times*, the Capitol City's daily newspaper, sat two men and a woman. The topic on this particular Monday of discussion was the current primary election campaign, and more particularly, the surprising emergence out of nowhere of Willie Hilton as a candidate for Attorney General.

Next to Edwin Martin, the Editorial Page editor, sat Orson Goldman who is the paper's political editor. The woman in the room was Kathy Christiansen, an associate editor and weekly columnist. Martin had been discussing the issues surrounding the volunteer group around Willie Hilton."

"I have never seen the emergence of such an incredulous following for a completely unknown candidate," said Martin.

"There are two factors here that may explain in the typical political jargon what is going on,' said Goldman.

"First of all, a lot of people are tired of the same politicians using the same rhetoric of promising solutions that never happen. Hilton is careful not to make any promises but he talks about being an 'outsider' who is frustrated that the same people who have been around for years and the same problems that have been around for years are still here. The same candidates are still asking the electorate to trust them because they have the experience to do the job."

Second, said Goldman, "Hilton is a new face that can resonate with an audience, especially the women. Neither of the other two candidates have any glitz about them. Right now all Hilton has going for him is his personality, but the voters are ready to gamble in the hope that he really will make a difference. Even with so little time before the election the momentum is all with Hilton."

Martin then asked for my opinion "I have to agree with Orson," said Kathy. "I am still perplexed at the way Hilton has created such a broad based volunteer army in so short a period of time. From what I can learn the Springville Foundation has something to do with it but I have yet to find out the details. But Orson is spot on when he says that the momentum is with Hilton. If he can get the funding to keep up the momentum he could walk away with the nomination."

Martin did not respond immediately but remained silent in deep thought. Finally he said to us, "All right. Let's find out everything we can about Hilton and who is behind him. We will not be making an endorsement in the primary but we cannot be caught asleep if he becomes the nominee. The Attorney General of the most populous state in the nation is by definition a national figure to be dealt with."

2

"BE SMART AND WE WILL TAKE CARE OF YOU!"

It had been two full days since Jezebel had wired the thousand dollars to the "investment advisor" who had called. The "voice" had promised her that a buyer for the option would phone her two days after she had paid the thousand dollars.

Once again the doubts and the anxiety were taking their toll. The media was now creating their own answers as to how Willie had zoomed into being almost even in the pre-election polls with two individuals who had a collective twenty-five years of experience in the State Capitol. Willie's campaign was desperately in need of a major media blitz. It was literally

coasting forward out of gas and in neutral gear. The small donations that were coming in did little more than keep the phones
connected, the campaign office rented, and gas in Willie's car.

Early on the morning of the third day the call finally came.
The caller ID showed a name she did not know from a secu-
rities brokerage in Switzerland. "Mrs. Hilton," the caller began,
"I understand that you have an option to purchase some cattle
that our firm would like to buy from you for one of our clients.
Do I have the right party?"

"Oh, yes, "said Jezebel, her adrenalin now increasing the
frequency of her heart beat by a factor of three times.

"I assume that you have the option electronically. Are you
able to forward it to me?"

"Yes," said Jezebel. Although she had never previously dealt
with futures options she understood the basics of how they
worked. "Where should I send it?" she asked.

The caller gave her the e-mail address and then said: "As
soon as I have received the option with your endorsement on
it we will be making a direct deposit into your bank account of
one hundred thousand dollars. Is that satisfactory?"

"Yes, of course," replied Jezebel. Then as the caller was about
to hang up she asked, "May I inquire as to who is your client?"
The caller was very appropriate but very brief and simply said,
"We never disclose to a seller who our client may be for fear
that the information could be used to manipulate the market.
The United States SEC (Securities Exchange Commission) does
not like that." With that the caller hung up.

Jezebel immediately realized that she had made a clumsy
mistake. At the same time she did not bother to wonder how
the caller knew where her personal bank account was located
and the account number. "Damn it, " she said, "How could I
have been so stupid."

Now the stress returned but not the adrenalin. "What if they
decided not to send the money because of that totally inept
question? How could I have been so stupid?" she asked. For

the next four hours she agonized and kept repeating to herself, "How could I have been so stupid."

Just after 1:00 p.m. the bank phoned. "Mrs. Hilton?" the bank officer asked?

"Yes," said Jezebel.

"We just wanted to let you know that a deposit just came into your account for one hundred thousand dollars. Would you like us to move the funds into an interest bearing account?"

"No, thank you," replied Jezebel. This time she did not ask where the funds had come from.

Now the adrenalin did begin to flow. She returned to her campaign strategy memorandum to look at what she had concluded would be the best media buy. Unfortunately that strategy had been developed on the assumption that there would be a full month before the primary election to implement it. Now there were just barely two weeks left before the election. It would be impossible to get bill boards designed and printed in less than a week, let alone rent whatever bill board spaces were available.

Once again she phoned John Vincent. As soon as he answered she said, "I can return your thousand dollars today if you would like."

"Really," he said. "What happened?"

"Some friends came through with a small five figure donation," said Jezebel, for whom the opportune lie was a well ingrained part of her nature. "But I do need another favor."

"What is it," asked Vincent.

"I need to be able to talk to someone who knows about political media advertising," she said. "Do you know anyone that will help me?"

"I know just the guy," replied Vincent. "He used to be one of the Governor's key campaign people but they had a falling out. I'll give him a call if you like."

"Please do," said Jezebel. Then as an afterthought, "Shall I just put your check in the mail?"

"That would be great," said Vincent. "I'll get back to you as soon as I can reach him."

In less than twenty minutes John Vincent phoned back.

"Hi. I just had a great conversation with Terry McNitt. Terry was on the Governor's re-election committee four years ago but they had a parting of the ways. He did most of the media buying for the Governor's campaign. But the really fascinating news is that he has been watching Willie's campaign and thinks that you have a real chance of winning. He would love to meet with you."

"Give me his number and I will call him right now," said Jezebel.

McNitt had assumed that the meeting would be at the campaign office. Jezebel told him that she could get more things done at home if she was not where the volunteers could interrupt her. He offered to come right over to the house.

McNitt was very similar to John Vincent. Very intelligent, very much an aggressive "make things happen" type of guy. He also had an effervescent personality that would fit right in as a key campaign operative.

When he arrived Jezebel was soon entranced by his sophistication with the realities of political campaigning. McNitt had his own public relations firm. However, Jezebel was astute enough because of her lawyer's training to ask a number of qualifying questions before getting to the issue of the media blitz.

McNitt answered all of the questions with charm but candor. He explained why he was no longer involved with the Governor. He had no other clients who were running for the A.G.'s office. His current political clients were seeking local State Senate and House seats.

In response to Jezebel's question about the cost for his services he simply replied that his personal fee would be quite "modest" as a consultant and that he would be earning a "commission" from the media entities from whom he was purchasing advertising for the campaign.

That issue then became McNitt's key question.

"How much are you able to spend?" he asked.

"Fifty thousand is all that we have?" replied Jezebel.

McNitt was silent for a few moments. "That's not much to work with," he said. Then he asked, "have you done any polling?"

Jezebel had not anticipated the question. "No," she said, "we couldn't afford any."

McNitt again was quiet as he mentally calculated whether or not he really wanted to get involved in what at this late hour in the election cycle probably would not be a success.

At this minute Willie came through the door. After introductions Willie was astute enough to tell that McNitt could be a powerful asset to the campaign. He turned on the charm and even though there was nothing to admire about Willie's integrity at least his personality was gold plated.

McNitt turned his attention back to Jezebel. "Let me tell you what I think it will take to win," he said. "You do not want to waste your media buy until you have done the polling that will tell you what your key message should be and who your primary target audience of probable voters would be. If you can come up with another twenty thousand dollars then for ten thousand we can get you a telephone poll that will define two or three key issues to be used between now and the election. The other ten thousand would be added to the fifty thousand you have in hand so that the total media buy would be sixty thousand dollars.

If you can do that I can give you a strategy for issues and media targeted to the right voters that will win the election."

Willie was about to ask the obvious question when Jezebel's kick to his shins under the table kept him silent. She could sense that in McNitt she had the professional public relations specialist that she desperately needed. McNitt for his part, having met Willie for the first time, was now instinctively betting that here was a horse that he could ride to victory in the primary and then get a high return on his investment in the general election campaign.

Jezebel looked straight into his eye and said, "How soon can you bring us the strategy memo and the media purchase schedule?"

"I can have it for you in the morning," he said. "But I need to know every place that you have held campaign meetings and what questions you have been asked."

"We can have that for you in two hours, " said Jezebel. "What time can we meet tomorrow morning?"

"I'll work on it this afternoon and tonight and be here by 8:00 a.m. tomorrow."

"It's a deal," said Jezebel. "We will have the list of the locations where we have campaigned ready by 6:00 p.m. How do I get it to you?

McNitt provided the standard contact information. Then as he was going out the door he turned and said, "Sixty thousand for media and ten thousand for the polling. Right?"

"Right" said Jezebel.

The door closed and Willie then said, "Are you insane? How on earth are we going to come up with seventy thousand dollars when we don't have a thousand dollars to our name?"

Here Jezebel's facility for instantaneous fabrication was put to the supreme test. What she did not realize was that the answer to Willie's question that she invented on the spot had far more truth in it than she realized.

"One of the people at the meeting in New York phoned to say that he had made some calls to people here that he knows They told him that if we could get some paid media there was a real chance of winning the primary election. He said to get back to him with what we need and he would do his best to help us."

Willie was euphoric. He immediately took out his pocket calendar and began to dictate to Jezebel every speaking appointment that he had filled for the prior six weeks. Jezebel phoned the campaign office to get some dates and places that Willie did not have in the pocket calendar. By six p.m. they had a complete list of locations where Willie had made a campaign appearance.

McNitt's request for the questions that people asked was more difficult. Willie had little interest in these questions but was skillful at responding with assurances that he could be trusted as the Attorney General to "make things right." Jezebel was even less useful in that regard having treated the campaign as a challenge in the technique of manipulating the electorate with Willie's personality and charm with little or no concern about a philosophy of government.

They finally had to admit to McNitt that most of the answers that Willie was using were pabulum for the politically unsophisticated. McNitt was not surprised that in fact there was no fundamental commitment by Willie and Jezebel to a philosophy of how government should function. There was no cause for which they were sacrificing in order to right a wrong or to protect the innocent victim. The only cause and the only motivation was to get Willie elected as the Attorney General. After that they could figure out how to use the office for their real objectives.

McNitt returned the next morning an hour late at 9:00 a.m. He had been up most of the night using sophisticated analyses of prior voting patterns and the socio-economic data from the last census. Just before mid-night he had finally contacted the pollster that he had used in the Governor's campaign four years earlier. He was now using that pollster for the three candidates for the state legislature who had retained his services.

When McNitt explained to the pollster who the client was the pollster was both perplexed and relieved. Perplexed because he was surprised that McNitt with all of his experience and success was involved with Willie Hilton. He was relieved because he had not been retained by either of the other two candidates for A.G. They in fact were using one of his competitors for polling in the state.

"Here's the deal," began McNitt. "With the names of the places where you have campaigned the pollster is going to probe for three things: first, what has been the reaction of those who have heard you speak; second; what do they want to hear from any candidate for the office of A.G. What are the issues that will resonate with what is important to them. Finally, we want them to compare you with the other two candidates, or more accurately stated, why would they prefer you or anyone else over the other two candidates."

"How long will this take?" asked Jezebel.

"We will get the results by early Saturday morning. He has put his entire team at our disposal, mostly as a favor to me, and because we can pay his fee up front. So when I leave here I will need to take him a check for the ten thousand dollars."

"Very well," said Jezebel. "Now what about the advertising—the paid media?"

"The content of the advertising will depend on what we learn from the polling," said McNitt. "But I have checked with the electronic media and they still have thirty second spots available. The printed media is a much more difficult situation. The daily papers have already committed the choice pages to other candidates. We will have to do something very creative in order to get the reader to stop and look at the ad for at least ten seconds. With so little money we many not bother with the newspapers."

McNitt then said, "I need to take Willie to a professional videographer's recording studio in order to get a thirty second tape that we can use for television. We will use the audio from the tape for radio. It will be the same message that will be used with the newspapers. We are going to find an issue that everyone will identify as having come from Willie—and that issue is going to win the primary election."

Jezebel wrote two checks for McNitt, one for the pollster and one for the videographer. With the checks in hand Willie and McNitt left to go make Willies' first television ad.

As Jezebel was dealing by telephone with the campaign office her phone rang. Again the caller ID was blank but Jezebel did not hesitate to take the call. As soon as she answered the voice said to her, "You have no idea how close you came to losing the entire deal with that question you asked yesterday. All you have to do is be smart enough to do what you are told and we will take care of you. What are you doing with the money?"

Jezebel recited the entire sequence from the phone call to John Vincent until the departure an hour earlier of Willie and McNitt. There was silence for almost thirty seconds which left Jezebel in a state of anxiety.. Finally the voice said, "O K. Make it happen." With that the connection went dead.

At the video studio McNitt had prepared a thirty second presentation for Willie. The studio had put it on a teleprompter. McNitt had Willie make three dry runs which he felt were satisfactory. The producer was genuinely complimentary of Willie's stage presence before the camera. "He is really good," the producer said to McNitt. Everything was ready and at a signal from the producer the camera rolled.

Willie went through the script without a hitch. The producer stood just beyond the teleprompter so that he could give hand signals to Willie for the time. For the last ten seconds the producer had both hands in the air and would drop a finger as the seconds went by. However, as Willie was finishing the producer still had three fingers in the air. Willie, still looking into the camera said something that he had been saying at all of the meetings where he had spoken. He simply said, "I won't forget you."

As McNitt and the producer watched the video for editing McNitt waited for that last three seconds and Willie's throw away extra line that was not in the script, "I won't forget you."

As soon as they heard it the two men turned to look at each other and smiled. Willie had somehow generated a magic moment—something everyone in the world of public relations dreams of. "That is a keeper," said the producer. "That is an award winning take."

Instinctively McNitt knew that he was right. Something that no one would have ever guessed had just happened. Willie was a "natural" in front of a TV camera.

McNitt made the arrangements for thirty copies of the spot to be sent to his designated media buyer. Willie and McNitt left the studio to find a suitable restaurant for lunch. During lunch they talked about local sports teams, and then, as Willie was eyeing several of the female patrons in the restaurant, the conversation turned to women. After several minutes McNitt realized that he had just learned something very important about his candidate. He made a mental note to tell Jezebel that she needed to keep a tight leash on Willie or the whole campaign would go up in smoke with the first sex scandal.

That night and weekend everyone worked at least eighteen hours every day. As the results from the pollster came in McNitt learned another lesson about his candidate. People who had heard Willie speak thought of him as a crusader for the "forgotten" part of the population. Willie could ingratiate himself with an audience by instinctively becoming one of them, whatever their socioeconomic background may be. Again Willie's instinctive comment at the end of the thirty second TV spot came to his mind: "I won't forget you."

After reading the polling data and showing the spot to Jezebel the decision was made to make Willie's comment the campaign theme and the essence of the electronic media. There was no money for the newspaper ads. In the largest state of the union sixty thousand dollars was not going to buy much television. Again going back to the polling data and the federal census socio-economic profile of every census district in the state McNitt was able to use the funds for electronic media in those areas where Willie's commitment 'not to forget them' would resonate the strongest.

Terry McNitt was the single most essential factor in the campaign other than the voice that phoned Jezebel. Since no one but Jezebel knew about the voice McNitt was the acknowledged genius and strategist for the campaign.

When the media that the voice had made available began to hit the result was electric. Both of the other candidates for

Attorney General had been able to spend three and four times as much money as the Hilton campaign. Yet, it was the Hilton campaign that the political activists were discussing. It was fresh, unique, and did not include the outworn political euphemisms that were so typical of state wide campaigns.

In the office of Edwin Martin, the Editorial Page Editor, the Editorial Page editor for the *Capitol Times,* sat Orson Goldman, the Political Editor, and Kathy Christensen, an editorial page columnist and co-editor. They began and ended every week on Monday morning and Friday afternoon with this meeting. This was their usual Friday afternoon recap of the week. All three of them knew Terry McNitt personally, and were well aware that he had chosen to join the Hilton campaign as the publicist.

"Well, you can see Terry McNitt all over the place," said Martin. "In one week that campaign has moved from an amusing amateur hour to first place in the race for A.G. My guess is that if their momentum keeps going Hilton will win the primary."

"I can tell you right now," said Goldman, "that Hilton's ability to communicate with the forgotten people in the electorate is fantastic. From the moment his media buys started running he has dominated the political gossip."

"What bothers me," said Kathy, "is that we still know nothing about him. His law school record was not remarkable. His wife is regarded widely among those who knew them at the university as the brighter partner in the marriage. They have the Springville Foundation as their primary client along with some of the smaller charities around the state. I'm concerned that we may have a Frankenstein on our hands and we won't know it until it is too late."

"Kathy, you need to give him a chance," responded Goldman. "I have never been present where he has spoken, and there is no way that I will be able to before a week from next Tuesday, but I can tell you that the gossip at the cocktail hour and the barbershop buzz is confirming that we are watching the emergence of a true leader. I'm excited to see it happening. One thing is certain. Politics as we have known it around this state is in for a big change."

"I think Kathy has made an important point," said Martin. "He may be a true breath of fresh air but since we know nothing about him I want to have you dig into everything about his background. Go back to his school record at the university. Find out anything that you can about his family. When the campaign donation reports come into the Secretary of State I want to find out who his major supporters are. In the meantime, we just watch and wait for another ten days."

With the jump in public interest in the campaign Jezebel had to move herself from their home apartment to the campaign headquarters. There were too many important people coming to the campaign office for her to be able to stay shut away in their apartment.

On Tuesday, with the election just a week away, a man named Dan Lamberger came to the headquarters and asked if he could meet Willie. Willie was out on the campaign trail and so he was directed to Jezebel. After the usual amenities were exchanged Lamberger took a very fat envelope out of his briefcase and handed it to Jezebel. "I am in the bond business," he said. "Last weekend some of the bond brokers around the state met at my office to talk about the campaign. Without exception they were convinced that your husband is the best possible candidate for A.G. and they asked me to give this to you in their behalf."

Jezebel was not so naïve as to assume that bail bond brokers were just public spirited citizens that were drawn to Willie. At the same time she could see that the bills in the envelope that were visible were hundred dollar bills. "This is really wonderful of you, Mr. Lamberger," she said. "I know that my husband will want to meet you personally. Will you be able to come to our victory celebration next Tuesday night?"

Lamberger was effusive in his response. "That would be great," he said, "may I bring some of my associates with me?"

"Of course," said Jezebel. "It will be our honor to have you join us."

With that Lamberger took his leave. Jezebel closed the office door and carefully counted out fifty one hundred dollar bills. Other than the wire transfer from the voice it was the largest single donation the campaign had received. Since there were no checks the campaign could simple report the five thousand dollars as "miscellaneous cash contributions."

Just then Willie returned with John Vincent and Terry McNitt. Both John and Terry were members of a downtown business club of select young men on the rise in the state Capitol. Today was their monthly luncheon meeting. It was too late to get Willie on the program but the two of them did a great job of taking him around to meet the members. Ironically, the Chief Deputy to the Attorney General is also a member of the club but was absent with a campaign appearance.

As Jezebel recited the conversation with Dan Lamberger there was a noticeable lack of enthusiasm on the part of both Terry McNitt and John Vincent. Neither of them knew Dan Lamberger personally but both were instinctively suspicious about a bail bond broker spontaneously coming to the campaign headquarters with an envelope full of hundred dollar bills.

This was when both Terry and John learned a new lesson about Jezebel. "I could care less how he makes his money as long as its legal," she said. "We aren't campaigning to be elected as the Sunday School teacher of the year. If Lamberger is willing to put his money on the table he is welcome to be at the victory party and he is welcome to come to the headquarters whenever he wants. This envelope gives us the ability to take care of half a dozen unpaid bills and that is going to make it easier for me to get some sleep tonight."

There was no doubt among the three individuals in the room as to who was actually in charge of the campaign. However, Terry McNitt was still able to turn the issue to his advantage. "We don't have a campaign legal counsel," he said, "someone who can keep us from getting into trouble with the election code. As the only non-lawyer in the room I would be a lot more comfortable if we had independent legal counsel helping us stay out of trouble."

"Do you have someone in mind?" asked Jezebel.

"There is a guy who volunteered on the Governor's campaign four years ago as one of the campaign legal counsel. He at least knows what the statutes are that we need to keep in mind."

"I'll have to go back to my time sheets about the campaign," said McNitt. I can't remember his name at the moment but I am confident that I can find him."

Everyone seemed to agree. Later that evening McNitt called Jezebel. "I found that attorney's name," he said. "It is Webster Reno. He was about five or six years ahead of you in law school."

"Find out if he is interested," said Jezebel. "I would like to have him come by the office in the morning."

McNitt was not really fond of Web Reno but he was quite confident that he knew the election code as well or better than any other attorney in town. He also was quite confident that he understood why Reno had not been invited by the Governor to come back and work on the current campaign. Reno often made it clear that he could cover up most violations of the election code with plausible excuses.

Like so many of his profession who become experts on the subject of election statutes Reno was an expert in knowing what was lawful and what was patently unlawful but was never bothered about the difference between what was right and what was wrong.

"I'll take care of it, " said McNitt.

That night at his office Dan Lamberger sat with two young boys in their late teens who were known as Lamberger's "Z" boys because their names were "Zeke" and "Zach," shortened versions of Ezekiel and Zachary. The discussion was about some "deliveries" that the young men were to make that night. During the day they were runners for Lamberger's bail bond business, moving back and forth from the county jail with notices of arraignments being entered into the court docket. If a bond was set they made certain to give Lamberger's business card to the attorney who represented the defendants.

However, the "deliveries" with which they were concerned this evening had nothing to do with bail bonds. The materials being delivered were street drugs that Lamberger sold to various gangs throughout the state. A very careful record was kept of what had been previously delivered and how much was owed to Lamberger. Zeke and Zach had both been given small motorcycles to use while making their rounds regarding bail bonds. The local police knew who they were and always assumed that they were only carrying documents to the attorneys for various defendants.

Lamberger now gave each of them a list of amounts that were to be collected from each gang leader as they delivered the current week's quota of crack, cocaine, heroine, etc.

"I don't want any excuses this time," said Lamberger. "Come back with the money or tell them that I will have some special collectors knocking on their door at 2:00 a.m. in the morning."

With that Zeke and Zach each put a dozen packages of various street drugs in their bike saddle bags and left. It was near mid-night when they both had returned with the cash owed to Lamberger.

McNitt made contact with Webster Reno who had worked with him four years earlier on the Governor's campaign. "I've decided to work with one of the candidates for A.G. by the name of Willie Hilton," said McNitt. "I am satisfied that he has a real shot at winning. Would you be willing to take on the campaign as a client?"

After a thirty minute conversation between McNitt and Web Reno there was a commitment made to meet at the campaign headquarters the next morning.

When he hung up the phone McNitt spent several minutes trying to determine if he was in danger of destroying his career. He had known of Lamberger as a local bond broker who was interested in politics and always seemed to be hanging around state legislators and others in the state capitol. He had never heard anything about Lamberger to indicate that he was not honest. At the same time it is not a good sign when someone delivers an envelope with fifty $100.00 bills in it to a political candidate that he had never met.

McNitt was also less than sanguine about his decision to call Web Reno. However, at this stage of the political season any election code attorney who was better than Reno was already committed to some candidate for state or federal office. Reno was smart, understood the state and federal election code, and should be able to keep the campaign out of trouble for failure to comply with the law.

The next morning McNitt was at the campaign headquarters thirty minutes before Webster Reno was to arrive. "He is very smart," he told Jezebel, "and he knows the election code better than the people who wrote it. He does not exactly have a sweet personality, but he makes things happen."

Reno arrived on time. Willie was out with a couple of campaign volunteers passing out literature and doing a "wave and honk" stint at one of the busiest intersections in the City. McNitt and Jezebel outlined for Reno what was currently happening in the campaign. Reno asked for the names of the Campaign Chairman, the Treasurer, and the Finance Chairman. "You are looking at all three," said Jezebel, and the tone of her voice made it clear that it wouldn't matter who else was involved or what titles they had. She would be making the decisions.

"Is that a legal problem?" said Jezebel.

"There has to be a campaign treasurer–usually it is a CPA— although there is no requirement that the Treasurer be a CPA," said Reno. "There are a variety of reports that have to be filed and certified by the Campaign Treasurer. Do you want me to find someone for you?"

"No," said Jezebel, "we will take care of it. What else do we need?"

Reno reviewed for her the fundamental legal requirements for the campaign. As they were talking a campaign volunteer knocked on the door. "Hey, we just saw an ad for Willie on TV It looked great. He was fantastic."

McNitt and Jezebel smiled at each other. They then turned to Webster Reno. "How do you usually arrange your compensation in a campaign?" asked Jezebel.

Reno was astute enough to know that he now wanted to have the Hilton campaign for a client. His conversation of the previous evening with McNitt had left him sharing McNitt's sense of intrigue with the campaign. "Why don't we do this, " said Reno, "I will just volunteer my time until the primary. Then we can talk about a specific financial arrangement for the general election."

Avoiding a decision about paying money was quite acceptable to Jezebel. There followed a lengthy discussion about the campaign strategy as McNitt had created it with Jezebel. When that was over Jezebel looked at Reno and asked if he needed an office at the headquarters. Reno said that he could function from his own office just fine.

Then McNitt and Reno left to get some lunch and Jezebel turned to the mounting stack of phone messages on her desk. "This sure as hell better work," she thought. "I don't intend to spend the rest of my life coddling buffoons so that Willie can have a job."

3

A NEW WORLD—A NEW LIFE

Election day had come. Willie was just opening the door to be on his way to meet Terry McNitt when Jezebel slammed the door in front of him and looked him dead in the eye.

"Listen to me," she said with lips tightly drawn and eyes aflame. "If you do one thing today to screw this up I will kill you. We have been damn lucky so far with your philandering. I don't want you to take one drink today until the final vote is counted. I don't want you talking to anyone without McNitt standing at your elbow. . . and I want to know where you are and what you are doing every minute of the day."

Willie's first reaction was to tell her how much he despised her and to make it clear that he would decide what he would do and who he would talk to and when he would take a drink. He calmed himself enough to keep his composure and simply said, "I'll see you at 11:00 when we go vote." With that he opened the door and slammed it behind him.

The independent polls taken the prior weekend showed Willie and the Judge in a "neck-and-neck" tie with the A.G.'s Deputy significantly behind them, Jezebel's stealth campaign against him had been incredibly successful. Most amazing of all, no one ever was able to trace the negative assertions back to Jezebel.

McNitt had arranged for the media to be present when Willie and Jezebel voted. They had originally planned the victory celebration to be at the campaign headquarters, but almost immediately it became obvious that a larger place would be needed. McNitt had been able to persuade the manager of one of the second tier hotels in the Capitol to give them a line of credit for the ballroom and the food and drink that would be served for the volunteers.

After Willie and McNitt had gone to the Democratic Headquarters to pay their respects to the State Chairman and the entourage that the Governor had installed in the headquarters they made a courtesy stop at the *Capitol Times*. McNitt had coached Willie on what to say and how to say it if they were able to meet with Orson Goldman.

After introducing themselves to the secretary who informed Goldman that they were in the outer office Goldman came out of his office to greet them. He had never met Willie before that moment.

Goldman knew Terry McNitt from other campaign and greeted him first. Then he turned to Willie and said, "Your campaign has been remarkable. I have to tell you that I have never seen a political novice gain such momentum so quickly."

Willie was appropriately modest and then said, "We hope that you can take a moment to come by out victory party tonight." Goldman was gracious and explained that he had promised the Governor that he would come to his event but that he would do his best to accept Willie's invitation.

When it was obvious that Goldman would not be inviting them to come into his office McNitt explained that their schedule was tight and they would need to get over to the voting location for the Hilton's. With that they departed.

After their departure Goldman stopped at Kathy Christiansen's office to tell her of the conversation. "He is no dummy," said Goldman. "Whether he is qualified to be the A.G. can't be confirmed right now one way or the other. I hate to admit it, but my first impression is quite positive. How about coming with me tonight to the Governor's reception and then going over to Hilton's party?"

After some momentary pause to see if she really wanted to leave the jeweled crowd at the Governor's reception for Willie's event Kathy finally agreed.

Kathy had good reason to be hesitant to accept Goldman's request. The real important people in the state would all be at the Ritz Hotel. The Governor's opponent in the primary was one of the state Senators who had opted not to hire McNitt even though he was intimately familiar with the Governor's campaign people. Neither Jezebel nor Willie as yet understood how important that decision was in terms of making it possible for Willie to hire McNitt.

By 5:30 p.m. people were already gathering at the Willie Hilton election night Headquarters. It soon became obvious that the campaign had way underestimated the size and the appetites of the crowd that had filled the headquarters by 6:30 p.m. The polls would not even close for another hour and a half.

For Jezebel it was a bitter-sweet moment. The size and enthusiasm of the crowd was a great omen for them. The volume of food and drink being consumed was way beyond anything left in the bank after the intense spending during the last ten days of the campaign. As she stood with Willie savoring the enthusiasm of the crowd Webster Reno came over to them.

"Congratulations, Willie and Jezebel," he said, "this is a great night. May I take just a moment and introduce to you one of the smartest political operatives I have ever met, Stuart Livingston."

It was not an opportune moment for Willie and Jezebel to accommodate Reno's request. They politely acknowledged the introduction just as Terry McNitt came to lead them away to meet some of the most powerful functionaries in the State Democratic party apparatus.

The polls closed at 8:00 p.m. The absentee ballots had been counted electronically and were posted by 8:30 p.m. As the voting results began to filter in the Judge took a significant lead over Willie. McNitt's analysis had predicted this because the first votes to be counted after the absentee ballots were in the Capitol city. But in a state with over thirty million people the results for the first ten percent to be counted would not be reliable enough to make any forecast. McNitt's professionalism and reliability kept Jezebel and Willie confident if not calm and comfortable.

Just before 11:00 p.m. a strange thing began to happen. Results from those areas of the state where McNitt had placed his sparse media budget were coming in and Willie was climbing out of the deficit that had developed over the prior three hours. All of the votes from the Capitol where the judge was well known had been counted. Those communities where Willie had campaigned personally and where McNitt had effectively used Willie's ". . . I won't forget you" thirty second TV spot were giving Willie a two to one lead over the Judge and a five to one lead over the A.G.'s Deputy.

By mid-night the newcomers to the party were not the "forgotten" blue-collar folks who drove ten year old automobiles. The CEO of the Springville Foundation who had left the Governor's party when the Governor's victory was assured came through the door with his wife. More and more of the elite party members started showing up as word spread that an upset was taking place in the A.G. race.

McNitt was making certain that Willie was available to shake hands with the "movers and shakers" from inside the Capitol city. However, one newcomer that McNitt had never met did not bother to go meet Willie. Dan Lamberger walked to Jezebel who was quite willing to welcome him.

After a few minutes of visiting while a hundred- fifty people were within earshot Lamberger asked Jezebel if he could take a moment of her time for a private visit. Just at that moment the TV coverage by one channel announced a projection that Willie Hilton had won the Democratic Primary. The ballroom burst into applause and cheers. In the midst of that distraction Jezebel led Lamberger to a private meeting room that the campaign had reserved for such purposes.

"I know that you need to go be with your husband," said Lamberger. "Win or lose we wanted to come and show our support for Willie. Our Political Action Committee board authorized me to bring you this check for $25,000.00." As Lamberger said that he took the envelope from his pocket and handed it to Jezebel. At that same moment another burst of applause and cheering erupted from the ballroom.

"Call me tomorrow afternoon," Jezebel said.

"How about 3:00 p.m." said Lamberger.

"Perfect," said Jezebel.

With that Jezebel put the envelope into her fashionably small jeweled purse and hurried back to the ballroom.

"I've been looking all over for you," said McNitt. It's time for you and Willie to make a victory statement." With that McNitt led Jezebel to the podium where Willie was waiting. Behind

Willie on the podium was Webster Reno with his new candidate for a position in the campaign, Stuart Livingstone.

Standing in the back of the crowd were Orson Goldman and Kathy Christiansen. As they listened to the victory speech that McNitt had rehearsed with Willie their thoughts and feelings were remarkably opposite although not vocalized. "Well, Kathy," Orson said, "a new star has just burst upon the political horizon. My guess is that we have just seen the beginning of a political career that will make history."

Kathy remained silent. As she listened to Willie's carefully crafted victory announcement her political instincts told her that Goldman was probably correct, but the consequences were far from clear.

As Willie and Jezebel finished speaking acknowledging the applause of the crowd they moved to the steps down to the ballroom floor. A man who was unknown to McNitt stepped forward and threw his arms around Willie.

It was Roger Hilton, Willie's younger brother.

4

THE WHEELS OF JUSTICE GRIND SLOWLY

Willie had barely won the primary election thanks to the strategic skill of Terry McNitt and the funds made possible by the unknown voice. As the Democratic Party nominee Willie had a new status in the state and with the media. When he and McNitt met the incumbent A.G. he was appropriately polite and cooperative but still harbored resentment over the defeat of his Chief Deputy by Willie.

Right after the primary victory McNitt accepted the title of Campaign Manager. He reserved to himself decisions about paid media. As he had promised Jezebel and Willie, his compensation came as a "commission" on the contracts that the campaign executed for radio, television, and newspaper ads.

Promptly at 3:00 p.m. the day after the primary election Dan Lamberger phoned Jezebel. His $25,000.00 PAC donation on election night convinced Jezebel to ask him to become the campaign finance Chairman. She did not see any need to consult Willie or Terry McNitt about this decision. Webster Reno became the chief legal counsel to the campaign with his ever present puppet Stuart Livingston given the title of campaign treasurer. It was made clear to Livingston that he was never to file any report about donors and the amounts donated without the express permission of Jezebel and or Reno.

McNitt was extremely nervous about having Lamberger as part of the official campaign leadership but decided not to make an issue of it. He was not fond of Reno but grudgingly admitted to himself that Reno knew and understood all of the legal requirements necessary to comply with the state election code. More important, he knew all of the tricks on how to violate the spirit of the election code without violating the letter.

Jezebel also chose not to inform McNitt that she and Reno decided to have Livingston organize and implement a harassment campaign of the Republican candidate's public appearances. Livingston recruited a cadre of college-age misfits who were compensated with alcohol and small amounts of cash. Livingston purchased a full sized outfit of a yellow barnyard rooster which he delighted in wearing at the Republican opponent's public appearances.

Two days after the Primary election victory Jezebel called a meeting of the key campaign people. The principle issue to be discussed was a budget for the general election and the fund raising process to finance the budget. Present besides Willie and Jezebel were McNitt, Lamberger, and Reno.

"I have calculated what it will take for all of the media," said McNitt. "We have thirty million people in the state living in five specific television markets. It is going to cost two and a half million dollars for a bare-bones media blitz around the state."

Knowing that Lamberger was in way over his head as the campaign finance chairman McNitt set out an initial strategy for fund raising. "We need ten fundraising events around the state," he continued, "except for the two here in the Capitol the others will need to net two hundred thousand dollars. Each of the two here in the Capitol will need to net double that amount. Direct mail is inefficient and expensive but we have to do it in order to get people used to Willie's name. There are half a dozen entities around the state that will want to have the contract. Dan and I will have to interview them and get the best deal possible. If we are lucky the response donations will about equal the cost of the mailings."

The broad outlines of a campaign structure that would actually get down to the grass roots in every county was next on the Agenda. Here the time that Willie and Jezebel had spent with helping local charities around the state became a golden source of volunteer and paid organizers.

During a break for coffee McNitt noticed Roger Hilton and Dan Lamberger engaged in a private conversation. Livingstone was detailed to find out what the two were discussing but as soon as he was within hearing range the conversation changed to generalities until Livingstone wandered off again.

After eight grueling hours of McNitt and Reno educating the others on the nuances of a state-wide political campaign in the largest state in the nation the meeting was adjourned for the rest of the evening. During the meeting the $25,000.00 that Lamberger had brought with him on election night had been committed for critical initial expenditures. Again McNitt noted that though they had come separately Roger Hilton and Lamberger left together.

Jezebel had left strict orders with the office staff that no one in the meeting was to be disturbed until it was over. One of the campaign volunteers named Jennifer Rose had been taking phone messages for Willie and Jezebel. She had been recommended to McNitt by Reno who confirmed that she had been a college intern in the Governor's campaign headquarters four years earlier. As soon as the all day session was finished Jennifer Rose brought in a stack of "critical" messages for both McNitt and Willie.

Even after the media interviews on election night very few people outside of the campaign headquarters had any idea that it was Jezebel who would be making the "critical" decisions. The messages were requests for media interviews, speaking appearances, applications for employment, etc. As Jennifer handed Willie his messages there was a brief but intense meeting of the eyes. She then returned to her desk in the main area of the campaign headquarters. One of the requests for employment that she handed to McNitt was her own.

Lamberger and Roger Hilton went to a favorite cabaret for dinner. After several drinks had been consumed and dinner was served Lamberger was able to assess that Roger Hilton was in fact a small supplier of street crack. By the end of the dinner Lamberger had recruited Roger Hilton into his own circle of drug runners.

Jezebel took all of the messages for Willie out of his hand before he had even had time to read the first one. "I will take care of these," she said. McNitt who had been getting about four hours of sleep a night since two days before the primary election excused himself and went home to catch up on some badly needed sleep. Willie desperately wanted to follow Jennifer Rose out to her desk but for once in his life suppressed his testosterone level and sat down across the desk from Jezebel.

They had gone through the first dozen messages when Jezebel's cell phone rang. She sensed that it might be the voice but she did not want Willie to even have a hint about the existence of the source for the one hundred thousand dollars that she had "earned" with her cattle futures option. However, the caller was persistent so she answered the phone.

"Are you alone," asked the voice.

"No. We just finished an all-day campaign meeting."

There was a pause and then the voice said, "make certain that you are alone in two hours." With that he hung up.

Willie and Jezebel continued to go through the messages that had come from all over the state and even from other parts of the country offering campaign services for fund raising and media design. Stuart Livingstone knocked on Jezebel's door and when invited in asked if the office people could go home for the evening. Jezebel now had the perfect way to get rid of Willie before the voice called back.

"Why don't you and Willie take them all to dinner," she said. Turning to Willie she said, "Use your Visa card to pay for dinner. When you come back you can take me home. Just be sure to bring me back something to eat."

"Great," said Livingstone. "There is a terrific Chinese restaurant in the next block." With that Willie and Livingstone gathered up half a dozen of the campaign volunteers, including Jennifer Rose, and walked down to the Chinese restaurant.

In exactly two hours from the time of the first call the voice called back.

"Are you alone," he asked.

"Yes," replied Jezebel.

"Tell me the details of your meeting. I want to know names and commitments."

Jezebel spent the next twenty minutes summarizing the decisions that had been made regarding Terry McNitt, as campaign manager, Webster Reno, as legal counsel, and Dan Lamberger, as finance chairman. McNitt's analysis of the essential budget issues for the campaign and the breakdown of the state in a structured organizational chart.

Unbeknown to Jezebel the voice had three other people listening to the conversation with ear phones. As Jezebel recited the names of McNitt, Reno, and Lamberger the voice nodded to one of the individuals wearing ear phones who immediately turned to a computer and started a background analysis of the person named. As Jezebel was finishing her recital of McNitt's campaign strategy and budget each of the three put a single sheet of paper on the table in front of the voice.

"McNitt is reliably straight," said the voice. "Lamberger is a petty drug dealer who is about to be indicted by the feds. Reno is competent but dirty and will have to be watched. "

Jezebel was stunned by the revelation about Lamberger. "We need this guy," she said, "other than you he is the only one that has come through with any funds."

"I'll see about delaying his arrest. But even so, Lamberger has no rapport with the type of people that you need around you. He has no ability to talk to the sources for the kind of money that you need. Don't make any more decisions like these without checking for my approval."

Jezebel clinched her jaws at being told so bluntly what she could and could not do. However, notwithstanding her instinctive recoil at the comment the memory of the one hundred thousand dollars kept her from losing her composure.

"Do you know the name Jim McFarlane?" asked the voice.

"No. I've never heard of him."

"He owns the Franklin savings and loan. He knows all of the seven and eight figure people around the state. He is going to be the Chairman of your two major fundraising events in the Capitol. And by the way, your budget is only one third of what it will take to elect your husband. Getting the real money that you need will be McFarlane's job."

There was another pause and then the voice said, "It may be too late to save Lamberger but let him go on with the other events outside of the Capitol. You will personally deal with McFarlane. You will hear from him shortly."

Another long pause and then this final word: "Do not ever try to record our phone calls. I will know the instant that you do and you will never hear from me again."

Jezebel stood and walked around the room. Her head was swimming with conflicting flash points—". . . your budget is only one third of what it will take to elect your husband . . . getting the real money that you need will be McFarlane's job . . . do not ever try to record one of our phone calls . . . Lamberger is a petty drug dealer . . . Reno is competent but dirty."

At that very moment Willie's brother, Roger Hilton, and Dan Lamberger were meeting with Zeke and Zach, Lamberger's runners. Lamberger had made an agreement with Roger to become a new distributor for Lamberger.

Willie and Livingstone soon returned, having sent the volunteers home. Jezebel just carried her Chinese restaurant take out to the car.

"Anything interesting in those phone messages?" Willie asked.

She was silent for a moment and then simply said, ". . . nothing really. Just a lot of people who want us to hire them."

Notwithstanding the adrenalin from the conversation with the voice her fatigue made certain that she quickly fell asleep.

Several days later Jennifer Rose brought a message to Jezebel that a Mr. Jim McFarlane was on the line asking to speak with Jezebel. As she took the call she remembered the warning by the voice not to attempt to record any of their phone calls. Nothing was said about phone calls with other people so Jezebel turned on the recorder that she had asked Livingstone to hook up to her phone.

"Mrs. Hilton," began McFarlane." My congratulations to you and your husband for a brilliant campaign. I have no doubt that he will be our next Attorney General."

A few more amenities passed between the two and then McFarlane said, "It would be an honor for me to have you and your husband be my guests for lunch. Is there a date soon when you could come to our office for a chat about the campaign." The office was on the top floor of a fourteen story building

A time was set for lunch on the top floor of the Franklin Savings & and Loan Building. When Willie and Jezebel arrived McFarlane introduced them to Clint and Tom, two individuals who McFarlane explained would be his key assistants in organizing the two fund raising events to be held in the capitol.

The first part of the meeting primarily consisted of McFarlane giving Willie and Jezebel a sales pitch on a pending land deal. Twenty-five miles west of the Capitol was a large lake that had been created by the construction of a reclamation dam across the path of two rivers. Franklin Savings and Loan was now in the process of acquiring a nine hundred acre tract that would be developed as the "Bluewater" housing project.

When the time came for the conversation to focus on the two fundraising events for Willie's campaign Clint and Tom made the presentation. They had been on the staff of one of the members of Congress from the State. Their duties included monitoring legislation taking place in Washington that affected the savings and loan industry, working with elected officials in both federal and state offices, and providing volunteer expertise to incumbent politicians for both federal and state office.

Clint and Tom outlined an approach for the two events that they had used in prior election years for the benefit of the politicians that were important to Franklin. The inevitable result was a very strong sense of indebtedness to Franklin on the part of these politicians. Clint and Tom were able to outline every detail of the two events, the individuals who would hold key positions in organizing the event, and the names of well-known Hollywood personalities who could be recruited to be the key attraction for the events.

At the end of three hours of discussion the key factors for both events had been resolved. Willie now had a campaign commitment to keep. He and Jezebel had driven to the meeting in their own car. McFarlane then volunteered Clint to drive

Willie to the campaign function leaving the Hilton's car for Jezebel to take back to the campaign headquarters.

After Willie and Clint had left and Tom had been excused to return to his office to prepare a memo for Jezebel to take back to McNitt outlining what had been resolved in their discussion with regard to the fund raising events McFarlane returned to the issue of the Bluewater Project.

"You know," he said, "that this will be an incredibly profitable project. I think that I could arrange for some financing for you and your husband to invest in Bluewater if you care to be partners in the development."

Jezebel was always open to a discussion about how to make money. "It sounds like it will be a sure winner," she said. "How much would we need to invest in order to participate?"

"Our partnership agreement requires a minimum investment of five hundred thousand dollars," said McFarlane.

Jezebel just shook her head. "I'm afraid that we are not in a position to invest anything like that amount," she said. "It sounds like a great opportunity but we will have to pass on it."

McFarlane just smiled and said, "Give me a few days to think about it and it may be possible to work it out."

McFarlane then showed Jezebel an empty office where she could make some phone calls while waiting for Tom to return with the memo for McNitt.

When Jezebel returned to the campaign headquarters with the memo she outlined for McNitt what had transpired. McNitt immediately called Reno at his office and with Reno on the speaker phone Jezebel recited what had transpired.

"Well," he said, "in the time that you were there you broke half a dozen federal and state election laws. McFarlane and his people must really want us to win this election if they are willing to run that risk. "

Jezebel of course had not mentioned to either McNitt or Reno the proposed investment in Bluewater that McFarlane had discussed with Jezebel. When Reno outlined the various illegalities Jezebel said, "What do you want me to do?"

"Just keep quiet about the whole thing," Reno said. "If they are that anxious to see us win then we will just have to make certain that insofar as we are concerned nothing was said or done that violates the federal and state statutes."

Later McNitt discussed the entire matter with John Vincent. Vincent was visibly concerned but opted to let Reno and McNitt keep everyone out of Jail.

As the two fund raising events to be held in the Capitol were being developed Lamberger was struggling with the other five smaller fund raising events for which he, as the Campaign Finance Chairman, was responsible. Jezebel informed McNitt that she would personally be responsible for the two events in the Capitol and that McNitt could spend whatever time necessary with Lamberger working on the five smaller events in other parts of the state.

The pattern that McFarlane and his two "government relations" experts used to promote the two large events in the Capitol city was quite simple. The CEO of a participating company would be contacted and informed that he would need to "sell" enough tickets to the event pay for five tables of ten people each. At $250.00 per person a table of ten people would cost $2,500.00. Five tables would net $12,500. The CEO would arrange to "find" the $12.500.00 in some uncommitted accounts and remit that to McFarlane as their "contribution" to the event. The CEO would then contact five junior executives and inform them that they were responsible to have four other couples in addition to themselves commit to spend the evening having an expensive dinner on behalf of a candidate that they had never heard of.

Three hundred tables for each of the two dinners in the state capitol would gross $3,750.000. After deducting the costs for the venue and the food the net to the campaign would be six million dollars. McFarlane and the Franklin Savings and Loan had pursued this strategy for many years resulting in a tremendous amount of political influence in both the state capitol and in Washington.

As McNitt attended the first of the two fundraising events in the Capitol he was overwhelmed with what McFarlane and accomplished. The next morning he doubled the campaign budget for media across the state.

While Jezebel, McNitt, and Lamberger were financing the campaign Lamberger and Roger Hilton were also increasing the scope and profitability of their association. Lamberger's "Z" boys, Zeke and Zach, were also recruiting some friends to act as "runners" for Lamberger's bail bond business as well as the night time work that Lamberger and Roger Hilton provided.

Because Lamberger was not competent nor qualified to successfully orchestrate the five smaller campaign fund raising events about the state McNitt found it necessary to leave the two larger events up to Jezebel while he managed the five smaller ones.

McFarlane had told McNitt that he had the"right" connections in Hollywood. McNitt decided to phone McFarlane and appeal for some help to find "star power" entertainment for his five smaller events. McFarlane made some phone calls to Hollywood and soon had a well known vocal artist committed to come with a small instrumental group. McNitt was struggling but he did make all five events profitable for the campaign although not nearly as much as what McFarlane made happen in the state capitol

At the editorial offices of the *The Capitol Times*, editorial page editor Edwin Martin, political editor Orson Goldman, and associate editor and columnist Kathy Christiansen were holding their weekly Friday afternoon recap of the events of the past week. They had finished their analysis of the Governor's race, the legislative races,, and now turned to the issue of the campaign for Attorney General. Martin turned to Goldman to make the first comment.

"I'm convinced that Hilton will be the next Attorney General. There is an atmosphere of success around his campaign. He continues to get good crowds at the fund raising events and the audiences are enthusiastic. If they can sustain their present momentum he will win. I'm also confident that he has become the most exciting candidate for state-wide office that we have seen in decades."

Martin listened and then turned to Kathy Christiansen. "Well, Kathy, have you finally come around to Orson's assessment?"

"Definitely not," said Kathy. "Hilton offers no solutions to the major issues for which the Attorney General is responsible. As near as I can tell he does not even understand the problems for which the state needs a strong A.G. I have to conceded that he gets fantastic crowds at all of his events. I keep asking why? As near as I can tell he has no core values, no philosophy that guides his campaign. He offers no vision of what he will accomplish in the next four years. In fact, as often as not when you listen carefully he just repeats what the Republican candidate has offered but with a slightly different twist to make it sound original with him."

Martin had the habit of putting his two hands together, palm against palm, and then using his hands to support his chin as he continued to evaluate what his two associates had said.

"What about the rumors concerning his sexual escapades? Is there any substance to those?"

"Look," said Goldman, "you have a handsome articulate man who has the gift for communicating to any group, large or small. He is the perfect target for that kind of rumor but so far no one credible has come forth."

"Kathy?" said Martin.

"I have heard the same rumors but they are not the sort of thing that anyone believable would state in public. If there is something going on I would think that his wife would soon find out. She is really the hammer in the campaign structure. It would be hard for Willie to be carrying on without her finding out about it. It is also impossible to conceive that a woman of that strength of character would tolerate anything like that from her husband no matter what office he held.

Actually, I'm not certain that anyone cares anymore about a candidate's moral values. Why should we be any different from the constant series of sexual escapades in Washington. The electorate just shrugs their shoulders."

Willie and Jennifer Rose had found a way to engage in an ongoing affair that even Jezebel did not suspect. One or two of the paid campaign staff were fairly confident that they knew what was going on between Willie and Jennifer, but as Kathy observed, "so what."

With just another week to go before the election Web Reno came into Jezebel's office at the campaign headquarters. "I have been contacted by the leaders of the State Employee's Union. They are prepared to put three thousand state employees at our disposal on election day as 'Get Out The Vote' volunteers. I've talked to McNitt about it but he thinks it is too risky. He is correct that it is a clear violation of the state law, but even if the press gets wind of it, it will be too late to make any difference in the outcome. What do you want to do about it?"

Jezebel summoned McNitt to come to her office. His position was quite direct. "Allowing the state employees union to put their people on the street for a 'get out the vote' drive is just too risky. The Republican Party will have poll watchers at every voting site."

Jezebel shook her head and made it clear that she did not agree with McNitt. " If the Republicans try to make an issue of it we will just accuse them of bigotry, of keeping the minority voters from exercising their rights. We will have Willie make 'protecting the rights of the excluded' a key element of his public appearances next week. Over fifty percent of the state's lower level employees are black and Hispanic. If we make minority entitlement a campaign issue first they won't dare to respond with any assertion of political wrong-doing."

McNitt still made it clear that he disagreed but he had learned that when Jezebel decreed that something would be done her way it was pointless to argue. By now accusation and intimidation of the messenger were Jezebel's standard responses when anyone accused Willie of improper conduct.

For nearly a month two investigators from the Bureau of Alcohol, Tobacco, and Firearms from the Department of the Treasury had been tracking Lamberger's runners, "Zeke" and "Zack.." They were quite certain that the two of them were delivering street drugs for Lamberger and Roger Hilton. On the weekend before the election they picked up the "Z- boys" during one of their delivery runs. It did not take the ATF people long to convince Zeke and Zach that they would be far better off if they agreed to cooperate with the federal agents by gathering evidence against both Lamberger and Hilton

When election day came the public opinion polls showed that in the A.G. race the two candidates were neck and neck. At Jezebel's insistence Livingston was put in charge of coordinating with the Democratic Party and the public employee unions.

The union leaders were more than able to mobilize nearly three thousand "volunteers" to round up stray citizens who had not voted. The State legislature had enacted an amendment to the election code providing for County Clerks to issue "provisional" ballots to anyone who came to the polling place asking to vote even though they were not registered. The election officials were to give them a form to fill out with their name and address. They were then given a ballot but the ballots were not to be counted until the County Clerks verified that the person was actually a resident at the address they put on their application.

During the afternoon and early evening of the election day the public employees brought in over five thousand individuals who were not registered to vote. Many of these were actually itinerant homeless street walkers. When the polls closed at 8:00 p.m. the Republican candidate had taken a healthy lead over Willie in the tabulation of the absentee ballots.

At the instruction of the Secretary of State, the senior election official in the State, the County Clerks were authorized to count of the "provisional" ballots without any verification that the name and address of the unregistered voter coincided with the actual facts. A post election survey of those ballots showed that more than ninety percent of them were cast for Willie Hilton.

At 11:30 p.m. these "provisional ballots" were certified as valid even though the Republican poll watchers had challenged them because no effort had been made to verify the name and address of the voter. Two hours later, by 1:30 a.m., the Secretary of State declared that Willie Hilton had been elected as the Attorney General.

5

THE SPOILS OF VICTORY

Under the State Constitution the Attorney General is the primary legal counsel for all of the state Agencies. As the Attorney General elect Willie appointed Webster Reno as the Chief Deputy Attorney General over the Criminal Division and John Vincent as the Chief Deputy Attorney General over the Civil Division. Soon after they formally took office Jezebel had Willie install Stuart Livingston as head of the Office of Personnel Security in the office of the Attorney General.

As soon as Willie took office Jezebel's presence and involvement with matters in the Attorney General's office was quickly established. All of the deputies and support staff became very conscious of the fact that although she had no title and no formal authority she did not need anyone's permission to walk into her husband's office and make use of any resources there, including any of the A.G.'s support personnel.

McNitt had decided to take a position with a public relations firm in Washington, D.C. As his final contribution to the Hilton's political journey he urged Jezebel not to take Livingston into Willie's personal suite of offices. They could find him something at one of the State Agencies. In a classic example of ingratitude Jezebel thanked McNitt for his concern and assured McNitt that she was quite able to deal with Livingston's burlesque handling of sensitive issues.

As one of her very first tasks for Livingston Jezebel had Willie sign a requisition for a new state of the art computer for Livingston's office. Over the next six weeks Livingston and Jennifer Rose entered the names and financial data of some twenty thousand people in the state, including data taken from their state tax returns.

Another of Livingston's assignments from Jezebel was to watch for a state bond issue that could be given to Dan Lamberger's agency for underwriting purposes. Just about mid-year Livingston and Webster Reno were able to arrange for a thirty-million dollar state bond underwriting contract to be awarded to Dan Lamberger's company for the underwriting. Lamberger in turn gave a "kickback" to Reno and Livingston of $5,000.00 each.

One of John Vincent's final client responsibilities before being formally sworn into office as the Chief Deputy Attorney General over Civil Affairs was to draft all of the documents for a loan of five hundred thousand dollars to Jezebel from a firm by the name of Investors Management Services. He also handled the documentation of Jezebel's investment into the Bluewater development as a member of the Bluewater Limited Partnership..

Using data gathered and provided by Zeke and Zach about the drug distribution enterprise of Dan Lamberger and Roger Hilton the federal Agents from the Office of Alcohol, Tobacco, and Firearms prepared warrants for the arrest of Lamberger and Roger Hilton. The night before the federal agents were to make their arrests the two boys set out on their usual route for distributing the drugs to various gangs in and around the State Capitol. When they did not return at the usual mid-night hour Lamberger sent out a "missing persons" notice through the Capitol City Metropolitan Police. At 3:00 a.m. the next morning their bodies were found on the railroad tracks. This in turn leads to Willie's first scandal in office.

The state Medical Examiner finds that the two boys had both received several stab wounds as well as multiple cuts and bruises from a heavy metal object such as a tire iron. As she is preparing to issue her finding that the boys were victims of a drug war she is summoned to the office of Webster Reno. Jezebel is sitting at the conference table as well. After an hour of intense intimidation by Reno and Jezebel she changes the death certificate for the two boys to read that their deaths were "accidental due to injuries suffered when they fell asleep on the railroad tracks after smoking Marijuana."

After the deaths of the two boys whose testimony was critical for the federal case the federal agents stopped working on the case. However, a report printed in the *Capitol Times* written by Kathy Christiansen forced Willie as the AG to instruct Webster Reno to assign a prosecuting attorney to investigate the matter further.

The deputy A.G. assigned to the case by Webster Reno is Elayne England. In her investigation she becomes aware that a low flying aircraft was used to drop drugs to the two boys. As she is looking into other issues involving their deaths she is removed from the Case by Webster Reno. Shortly after that she resigned as a Deputy Attorney General. On the day before her departure from the state she gives an exclusive interview to Kathy Christiansen of how she had been harassed and bullied by Reno with regard to her investigation.

At the end of the calendar year Willie requested the state legislature to give the State Medical Examiner a thirty-two thousand dollar raise. After some intense negotiation between Willie and the legislative leadership the legislature cuts the request in half to sixteen thousand dollars and passed the bill.

Shortly after Willie had taken office there was a discovery of a substantial deposit of Uranium ore on the lands reserved to the state when it was admitted into the union. These lands were specifically designated for the support of the public schools. Any exploitation of minerals on these lands was to be negotiated through the office of the Attorney General with a certain percentage of the proceeds to be deposited in the State school funds.

When this discovery is announced the Voice informs Jezebel that it is important that the State not enter into any arrangements about mining the uranium until Jim McFarlane contacts Willie on behalf of a Canadian business man by the name of Arnold Tucker. Several days later Willie gets a call from McFarlane about having a meeting at his office with Tucker. McFarlane explains to Willie that Tucker has huge ore mining holdings in Western Canada which include substantial uranium deposits. McFarlane brokers a private luncheon for Willie and Tucker at his office on the top floor of the Franklin Savings and Loan.

At the end of the luncheon Tucker invites Willie to come to his hunting and fishing lodge in Canada later in the summer. Willie agrees and Tucker sends his private jet down to the state Capitol to pick up Willie. Jezebel opts to stay at home.

In Tucker's private jet Willie travels to the Lodge in early August. Tucker takes Willie out to a favorite fishing hole and Willie easily catches a dozen trophy trout. For the remaining two and a half days at the Lodge Willie opts to remain in the theater room of the lodge watching Tucker's library of pornographic movies.

Back at the Capitol the Governor had been invited to participated in an exchange program with industrialists in Japan sponsored by the U.S. Department of Commerce. Governors of the several states would go on an exchange visit to Japan looking for opportunities to market products manufactured in their state. The Japanese in turn would send a delegation looking for opportunities for Japanese products to be sold in the U.S. and for Japanese companies to establish a manufacturing base in the U.S.

Quite predictably the Governor and the entourage traveling with him did not have any success in finding a possible market in Japan for any of the products produced in the State. However, one of the Japanese entities scheduled to participate in the return visit had sent a letter to the Governor requesting an opportunity to discuss an exclusive license to build a uranium refining and concentrating facility near where the Uranium deposit was discovered.

The Governor sent the letter over to the office of the Attorney General for follow up with a copy to the office of the Director of State Lands. Willie gave the letter to John Vincent.

Jezebel was instructed by the Voice to make certain that when the reciprocal visit by the Japanese industrialists was scheduled that someone Jezebel could "trust" be assigned to coordinate the visit. That person's responsibility would be to make certain that Jezebel would know all of the details of the Japanese proposals. Jezebel requested that Vincent detail Stuart Livingston to be the contact person for both the State officials and the Japanese delegation. Vincent reluctantly accommodated Jezebel's request but also assigned one of his deputy attorneys to work with Livingston.

Livingston was more than equal to the opportunity. He made certain that he was involved with all of the exchanges of information that came to and went from the State to Japan. Since the Uranium deposit was on State School lands the Attorney General was the primary decision maker regarding any request to obtain a mining lease for the deposit as well as deal with the proposal to grant a license for construction of a uranium refinery and a concentrator.

Livingston's contact with the Japanese company was with a man named Yoshihiro Kato. Kato could speak and write excellent English. Livingston sent him a self-serving memo in which he introduced himself as the officially designated contact with the company. As the time drew closer for the delegation from Japan to arrive Livingston took occasion to mention Jezebel by name as the "official" hostess for the delegation. Since the Governor's wife had not had a pleasant experience in Japan she was more than happy to yield that designation to Jezebel.

John Vincent and the deputy A.G. assigned by Vincent to work on this matter were always copied on Livingston's memos to Japan. Jezebel was brought into the planning process to make certain that the appropriate courtesies were extended in terms of meals, entertainment, accommodations (for which the Japanese would pay) and sight-seeing.

The State hosted a banquet on the first night of the delegation's visit. Kato had asked Livingston to make arrangements for Kato to have a brief private meeting with Mrs. Hilton. At an appropriate time during the evening Jezebel, Livingston, and Kato were able to make use of an adjoining office. There Kato, with perfect English, thanked Jezebel for all of the kind efforts that she had put forth on behalf of the delegation and then asked her to accept a red envelope as an expression of their gratitude. Jezebel thanked him for the gift and promptly handed it to Livingston.

Livingston put the envelope in his briefcase and they returned to the dining room.

At the end of the evening's festivities Livingston presented to each member of the delegation a binder that contained all of the details for the ensuing five days. Livingston had also requested of Kato that he be allowed to put into the binder the details of the proposal that the Japanese would be making regarding mining and refining the uranium. Kato responded to Livingston's request. Jezebel then scanned the Japanese proposal and forwarded it to the Voice.

Jezebel also presented a very expensive gift to the wives of the members of the delegation that she had selected, which was paid for by the state.

The next day Livingston and Jezebel boarded the tour bus with the delegation. Jezebel made certain that every appropriate courtesy was extended. Livingston and a man from the State Lands office conducted the tour with Kato acting as the interpreter. When the five day tour was over the Japanese delegation left two of its members, one of whom was an attorney who had done advance studies in American Law at the University of California. Their mission was to negotiate with John Vincent.

At the farewell dinner hosted by the Japanese another brief private meeting with Jezebel and Kato and Livingston took place. Another red envelope was presented to Jezebel in gratitude for her kind efforts on their behalf.

Within two days after the delegation's departure Jezebel's private bank account showed two cash deposits of $10,000.00 each.

In a conversation with the Voice Jezebel is informed that it is extremely important that the concession for the mining of the uranium go to the Canadian, Arnold Tucker. The Voice also informs Jezebel that Livingston is taking monthly payments from the Japanese to make certain that their interests in the uranium mining contract are protected.

When Jezebel becomes aware of Livingston's unauthorized advocacy on behalf of the Japanese she threatens him with banishment. He quickly terminates his interest with the Japanese which tips them off that someone else now has the inside track on obtaining the uranium mining concession.

Jezebel also now realizes that since Livingston is aware of her acceptance of the two red envelopes stuffed with hundred dollar bills he has the ability to reveal her unlawful acceptance of those "gifts." At the same time she forces Livingston to cease helping the Japanese Jezebel assures him that there will be another state bond contract for Lamberger's firm. At the same time Jezebel begins to think of ways to get rid of Livingston.

Willie's brother Roger was not the only family member attorney to ride the Hilton Train to the State Capitol. Jezebel's brother, Paul, had graduated from one of the private non-accredited law schools in the state. After his graduation he was finally able after two failures to pass the State Bar and land a position with one of the smaller counties in the state as a public defender.

During Willie's term as the Attorney General the highly publicized class action lawsuits against the tobacco industry were finally completed. These class action law suits were instigated by a variety of law firms across the country that had specialized in recruiting plaintiffs into class action law suits against large corporate targets. The fees that the court would award to the attorneys for the plaintiffs in the tobacco class action lawsuits would reach into the tens of millions of dollars

The Plaintiffs in these lawsuits had also been joined by many of the nation's state Attorneys Generals who executed contracts for their state to be represented by some of the law firms involved in the lawsuits. These law firms, as the plaintiff's lawyers, were clever enough to persuade Willie's predecessor to agree to a contingency contract that entitled the law firm to as much as a 25% of the state's share of the final settlement.

That final settlement for all of the plaintiffs was $368.5 billion dollars

The legal theory that the states used to assert their claims was the increase in public health costs that were related to tobacco use.

When it became evident that the settlement would include a huge financial bonanza for the law firms representing the states one of those firms invited Jezebel's brother Paul to become an "associate" in the firm. The final settlement details with each of the states would involve the office of the Attorney General. The potential settlement for most of those firms would be a payout of as much as or even more than fifty million dollars.

Given the fact that Paul had never represented a single plaintiff in a tort law suit let alone in a class action law suit of any amount, it was certainly remarkable that an attorney so deservedly obscure should overnight become a potential millionaire.

For the law firm that retained Paul twenty-five percent of the award to the State would come to well over fifty million dollars. If Paul's usefulness was nothing more than a defensive measure to keep the state from re-negotiating its claim with the law firms "to protect school children from Joe Camroel" he was well worth whatever he finally received.

As soon as Willie was elected Jezebel had hired a computer specialist to create her own private router and server. No one, not even Willie, had knowledge of the router. The specialist Jezebel hired was able to engineer the router so that it left no signature. Jezebel could send e-mails to anyone at any time but unless she specifically included her router ID there was no way for the recipient to know where the e-mail came from.

When Paul was retained by one of the Plaintiff's law firms in the Tobacco settlement he came to Jezebel to appeal for her assistance. He desperately needed to show that he was an "insider" insofar as the Attorney General's office was concerned.

Jezebel agreed to provide Paul with information as to how the deputy A.G. assigned to the case was developing his strategy in terms of the State's contract with the law firm. Willie was on the distribution list from that Deputy. The Deputy was in constant contact with the attorneys from the Plaintiff law firms. Paul's contribution to the law firm that retained him was to keep them advised of how Willie intended to deal with re-negotiating the twenty-five percent (25%) contingency fee that Willie's predecessor had agreed to.

Since Jezebel had open access to Willie's office and his "in box" of memos from various Deputies in the office she could easily find out what the Deputy assigned to the tobacco suit was recommending to Willie. Over a period of more than two months Jezebel would feed information to Paul that was of enormous benefit to the law firm in terms of their negotiating posture with Willie. By doing this Jezebel significantly weakened the State's ability to re-negotiate its 25% "contingency" fee contract with the law firm. If Paul was inept enough to let one of Jezebel's memos fall into the hands of the law firm there was no way that it could be traced back to Jezebel.

Indeed, Paul proved to be more than worthy of his compensation that was part of the judgment that the law firm received against the tobacco companies.

As previously noted, prior to Willie's election victory and his being appointed as the Chief Deputy Attorney General for Civil Affairs, John Vincent had done all of the paper work for Jezebel's investment of five hundred thousand dollars in the Bluewater project.

In their third year in office the Bluewater project by Franklin Savings and Loan was cited by the U.S. government's Federal Housing Administration (FHA) as a fraudulent real estate Ponzi scheme. Jim McFarlane and his wife were indicted along with several other participants including the firm and the CEO of Investor Financial Services. This is the firm that Jim McFarlane used to loan Jezebel the five hundred thousand dollars which she invested in the project. Jezebel's financial obligation for repayment of the loan to Investor Financial Services was covered by quarterly dividends from the Limited Partnership.

Jezebel's five hundred thousand dollars allowed the Limited partnership to show an increase of equity of five hundred thousand dollars. Those funds immediately went back to Investors Financial Services as a dividend from the partnership.

Thus without spending a dime of her own money Jezebel became a stakeholder as one of the Limited partners in a multi-million dollar real estate development project.

The Bluewater Project involved 900 acres of prime residential land along the shores of the lake that had been formed by the reclamation dam just twenty-five miles west of the state Capitol. The 900 acres were subdivided into 2700 lots, three lots to the acre. These lots were marketed as "second homes for weekend and summer vacations."

Franklin Savings and Loan in turn loaned funds to purchasers of the lots. These loans to purchase the lots were secured by a second mortgage upon the borrower's primary residence. However, Franklin Savings and Loan was committed in that sale to finance for the purchaser the necessary funds to construct a vacation home on the lot.

A significant downturn in the national real estate market forced the Limited Partnership into insolvency. Nearly a thousand of the lots had been sold based on the marketing credibility of Franklin Savings & Loan. The money that these purchasers had paid into the Limited Partnership was gone. Jezebel's quarterly dividends from the partnership by which her loan from Investors Financial Services was being repaid came from funds invested by the individual purchasers of the lots. Thus, as a partner in the Limited Partnership Jezebel was to be indicted for fraud.

Since the prosecution of the matter was with the federal government Willie was in no position to protect Jezebel as one of the partners in the Limited Partnership. As Jezebel was subpoenaed to testify before a federal grand jury the Voice directed Jezebel to an attorney in Denver who was the former attorney for Investor's Financial Services. His testimony before the Grand Jury included the assertion that in fact Jezebel had lost $68,000.00 as a member of the Limited Partnership.

The individual lot purchasers essentially lost eighty percent of their investment. After years of litigation and the appointment of a bankruptcy trustee to liquidate the assets of the Limited Partnership the lot purchasers were able to receive twenty cents on the dollar from the trustee. Because of her perjured testimony before the Grand July Jezebel was never indicted as one of the partners in the Limited Partnership even though as a partner she received a very substantial quarterly dividend for her phantom investment.

Thanks to the legal skill of John Vincent and the Voice's recruitment of the former Attorney for Investor's Financial

Services the ability to calculate Jezebel's fraudulent enrichment out of the Bluewater project could never be accomplished.

The Bluewater project's collapse was not the only "near miss" that Willie and Jezebel experienced. Willie had accepted a request from a very prestigious charitable organization in the State Capitol to be the featured speaker at a noon luncheon. The venue for the event would be the Ritz hotel one of the five star hotels in the Capitol.

Willie and his two security guards arrived at the hotel early and wandered around to the pool area. Lounging beside the pool in the briefest possible bikini was a local woman nicknamed "sweet Tammy Hinsey." In her journal which she faithfully kept on a daily basis Sweet Tammy confided that her' lifetime ambition was to "set a record of having sex with nationally prominent rock and roll musicians."

She was lounging beside the pool because that evening one such Hollywood rock and roll gang was to perform at the hotel. The promoter for the event had retained her services on behalf of the performers for after the "concert.' The promoter had also provided "sweet Tammy" with a luxury room for the night.

Willie spotted "sweet Tammy" in her shoe-string bikini and detailed one of the security men to approach her on his behalf. According to her journal entry a man "dressed in a business suit" walked over to her and simply said, "Willie Hilton would like to meet you." According to her journal entry she got up and followed the man into a remote hall of the hotel. There she was introduced to Willie who cut right to the heart of the matter by saying, "I would like to get together with you. Where can we go?"

The hotel room that she had been provided was still not cleaned and ready for use. She followed Willie down the hall as he popped his head into a few meeting rooms hoping to find an empty one where his state police troopers could stand guard. No such luck.

Willie finally settled for some oral sex in the darkened hallway as the security guards made certain that no one else would come down the hall.

Miss Hinsey's journals would be the source of an article in **Penthouse,** one of the nation's sex magazines. Unfortunately that is not the end of the story.

After Willie had given his talk the program chairman for the event appropriately thanked him. Her name was Juanita Fields. She and her husband were well known activists in the exclusive Capitol City social world. Using the pretext of needing to make a private phone call to his office he asked Mrs. Fields if he could use her hotel room. Somewhat taken aback by the request but presuming that the two security guards would also be present she consented to allow Willie to use her room. Inasmuch as her purse and other personal items were in the room she simply went with him to the elevator and up to her room.

Willie's brief but unsatisfying encounter with sweet "Miss Tammy" in the hallway had ignited his passions. Willie had the security detail remain outside. According to the exclusive interview which Mrs. Fields subsequently gave to Kathy Christiansen what happened next was literally a brutal rape. When Willie finally left her she was bleeding from her lips and her face was so bruised and swollen from being bitten that she literally went into shock.

When she had recovered from her trauma she attempted to reach her husband but to no avail. He was on the east coast on a business trip. She took her personal items and her satchel of papers and drove home.

When her husband called that night she was still unable to coherently describe the experience. She asked to be excused from the phone call because she was not feeling well and she just needed a good night's sleep.

It was nearly a year later when Willie had announced that he would run for Governor that she confided in her husband what had happened. His initial reaction was to find Willie and kill him. Having had an entire year to recover from the experience she appealed to him to just let this nightmare go away. He finally acceded to her request to just be allowed to forget what had happened.

During Willie's campaign for Governor Juanita Fields met Kathy Christiansen at a charity benefit event. The two became close friends. In the course of their friendship a time came when rumors of Willie's philandering with several of the females in the Attorney General's office and other women had become common gossip in the Capitol.

In a conversation between Juanita and Kathy the issue of Willie's various sexual escapades came up. After obtaining from Kathy an absolute commitment of non-disclosure, and with tears and trembling lips and hands, she confided in Kathy what Willie had done to her that day a year earlier. Just being able to tell someone besides her husband seemed to be a huge source of relief. Somehow sharing that experience with a sympathetic and loyal friend lifted much the terrible burden of guilt from her shoulders.

Juanita finally agreed to let Kathy use the story if Kathy did not disclose Juanita's identity.

After her heart wrenching conversation with Juanita about the rape Kathy was working on a special article about the increase of drug related crimes during the administration of Wllie Hilton as the Attorney General. She had several interviews with the special agents for the Treasury Department's bureau of Alcohol, Tobacco, and Firearms who are often referred to as "T" men.

Even though the investigation of the deaths of Zeke and Zach had been stymied by the ability of the Voice to deal with matters in Washington the "T" men continued to work on the issue of the distribution of drugs in the Capitol City. Thus she received a phone call from one of the "T" men informing her that the previous evening they came across Willie's brother Roger Hilton making a sale of cocaine. He was arrested and ultimately makes a deal with prosecutors by testifying against Lamberger. Both men served relatively brief jail sentences.

By this time in his political career Willie and Jezebel have perfected their "technique" for dealing with scandal. In the case of Willie's brother Roger their strategy is one of simply ignoring the reality. In the case of the Medical Examiner's initial determination about the deaths of Zeke and Zachary the strategy is one of intimidation and threatening. Then when the Medical Examiner revises the "cause of death "determination to one of overdosing on marijuana she is rewarded by Willie by having the legislature provide her with a hefty increase in her salary.

In the case of Dan Lamberger's conviction because of Roger's cooperation with the prosecutors Lamberger is given a pardon by Willie shortly after Willie is elected as Governor.

"Where will it all end?" Kathy asks herself. "Can it possibly get any worse?"

The murder of John Vincent proves that it can.

6

THE MURDER OF JOHN VINCENT

John Vincent had graduated from law school as the first in his class. He had been elected to the "Order of the Coif" which is the highest honor that a graduating law student could obtain. The Dean of the law school watched John's career with the largest law firm in the State Capitol and then his appointment as the Chief Deputy Attorney General for Civil Affairs with a sense of great personal satisfaction.

The law school had a tradition of inviting a former graduate back to speak at a black tie event known as "The Founders Forum." So it was that the Dean contacted John with the invitation to be this year's speaker at the formal dinner. As the Dean extended the invitation John was both astounded and at the same time delighted to have the honor extended to him. The two arranged for a private lunch in the Dean's office to discuss the details.

On the day of the luncheon John and the Dean discussed various topics for the title of his talk. During their discussion the Dean became somewhat somber as he recited the changes that he had seen in the legal profession since his becoming a faculty member some thirty-five years before.

"I have always regretted that First Amendment decision regarding advertising by attorneys and other professionals," he said. "Somehow it took away the sense of dignity and pride in the profession as one of the most noble pursuits open to an individual of high ideals. Instead of being an officer of the Court in the pursuit of truth the profession became one of skillful manipulation by using half-truths to justify an end." The Dean then repeated what John had often heard him say to the students, "Your integrity will be proven by your conduct. Integrity is truth in action. It is the essence of being a person of honor and virtue."

At the end of the lengthy discussion the Dean said, "John, whatever you decide to say I pray that you will instill within them the need to restore in the minds of all people their respect for the practitioner of the law as a person of honor and integrity."

As John drove back to his office at the State Capitol he could not help but ask himself whether or not he was really worthy to present such a message. For some time he had agonized over the ways in which his relationship with his cousin Willie and Willie's wife Jezebel had compromised the vision of his values and his personal integrity. As he raised the issue in the privacy of his home with his wife and others he was never quite satisfied that he had not allowed the allure of what others regarded as success to justify conduct by himself that he once regarded as reprehensible.

He worked intensely at preparing the talk. He wanted it to stand as a statement of truth that would instill the idealism that he felt about the law into the minds and values of those who would hear the talk.

His draft of the talk was on his computer at home. At night and on weekends he would return again and again to his manuscript in search of the wording that would indelibly capture the intensity of the way he once felt about being a practitioner of justice.

As John continued to revise and restate his message he was unaware that his computer data base had been compromised so that others knew everything that it contained from his daily journal to the most innocuous memo. Even before Willie had persuaded him to accept the appointment as Chief Deputy for Civil Affairs the so-called "fire wall of protecting his privacy" had been breached. Thus as John was preparing his "Founder's Day Talk" and refining his thinking about the issues of integrity and honor others were made aware in real time what was happening in his mind.

A week before the speech was to be given he wrote in his personal journal: "I have lost my way in pursuit of present achievements that have no lasting value. Before it is too late I am going to return to the vision that I have lost through the slow stain of the world."

The next day at his office he received a phone call from one of the members of the State's congressional delegation. At issue was a decision about the lease of the state lands that contained the uranium deposit. The caller asked John to meet with a man who John did not know but was represented to be an international expert with regard to uranium ore. The request was for a meeting away from his office in order to avoid any media awareness of the discussion. A small restaurant that was near the lake where the Bluewater project was to be developed was selected as a meeting place. Just after the lunch hour John left the office with a briefcase that contained his current files on the matter of the lease. He said nothing to his secretary about his appointment or when he would return.

As John pulled into the parking lot behind the restaurant a white delivery van with no windows except for the driver and one front seat passenger pulled into the parking place beside him. Two men emerged from the van and introduced themselves as the individuals who were to meet with him. They explained that in the back of the van was a spectrometer with some samples of the ore from the state lands. They asked to have him look at that before going inside the restaurant.

As the back door was opened and John looked inside he was struck in the back of his head and rendered unconscious. One of the two men pushed him into the back of the van where an aerosol can of mace was shot into his face and he was now totally unconscious. One of the men got into the driver's seat of the van and the other one, after obtaining John's car keys from his pant pocket, got into John's car. The van followed by John's car pulled out of the parking lot and proceeded down the road to the entrance of a dirt road used by fire fighters to obtain access to remote areas around the lake.

Walking along the lake shore was a young Hispanic couple. Her name was Annabella. She was a citizen working as a nanny for a wealthy family that lived by the lake. His name was Javier. He was an illegal alien who had been twice deported back to his home land. One more apprehension as an illegal alien and he would be sent to prison. Their conversation was about their prospective marriage.

They chose to sit in the shade of some trees and brush that were located between the lake shore and the fire fighter's dirt road. As they were talking the van pulled up behind the trees and brush and John's car pulled up beside it. They could not be seen from the vehicles. As soon as the two vehicles were parked they heard a muffled gun shot from inside the van. As he looked out through the brush Javier could see the two men drag a third man out of the back of the van, lay him on the ground beside his car and place a revolver in his right hand. Both men then got back into the van and drove away. Javier dictated to Annabella the license plate number of the van.

After the van was gone Javier told Annabella to sit very still and wait for him. Annabella had been carrying a Kodak disposable camera on their walk. He took the camera, went through the brush to the road and photographed John who was lying face up beside his car. Javier took several photos of the surrounding area. The couple immediately started back to the home where Annabelle was a Nanny.

As they walked Javier explained to Annabelle the consequences if he were to make contact with police about what they had seen. He would immediately be arrested and most likely become the number one suspect for the murder. This time he would not be sent back home but would be put in jail until a decision was made about his personal involvement in what they had seen. He assured Annabelle that he would report what they had seen. She was not to mention it to anyone.

Javier waited for the bus to come that would take him back to his own neighborhood. On the bus he found a copy of the *Capitol Times*. He took the paper and the disposable camera to his home. He put some surgical gloves on his hands that he had taken from the medical clinic where he was one of the cleaning crew. Making certain that there were no fingerprints on the camera or the box he took a small box of candy, disposed of the candy, and put the camera in the box. He also put into the box a piece of waste paper upon which he had written the license plate number of the van. He wrapped the box in some brown paper and then addressed it to "The Editor" of the *Capitol Times*.

Again using the bus he went to the inner city of the State Capitol. By this time the Post Office was closed. Using the automated stamp machine he determined how much it would cost to mail the box. Affixing the stamps he deposited the box into the outgoing mail slot. Since it was after the last dispatch from the post office the box would not be sent out with the mail until the next day.

Although she was often at the Attorney General's office Jezebel had not been so presumptuous as to have an office there assigned to her. She simply walked into Willie's office and used the conference table there. It was now late afternoon when her new cell phone rang. Her instincts told her that it was likely the voice. She answered softly. His message was succinct and brutal.

"Your friend Vincent is dead. He was getting ready to go to the press about your loan. You must get all of your files out of his office and get them hidden until there is time to go through them. Don't bother asking me any questions. Just understand that if those files get examined by the police you and your husband will be going to jail."

With that she heard the click that ended the call.

For a few minutes she was paralyzed with shock. Then literally leaping from the chair she rushed to John Vincent's office.

"Where is he?" she demanded of the secretary.

By this time all of the support staff in the office of the AG knew better than to question or to challenge Jezebel. If she sensed any lack of respect or doubt about her authority it could be fatal to one's career.

"He left just after lunch," said the somewhat startled secretary.

"Where did he go?" demanded Jezebel.

"He did not tell me where he was going. He asked for the files on the uranium matter and left."

She returned to Willie's office. Using her cell phone she called John Vincent's number. No answer. The time now was 4:30 p.m. She decided to wait until Vincent's secretaries had left before going back to his office. With trembling hands and a highly accelerated heart beat she sat silently. For once she wished Willie was present but he was gone until later in the evening.

At last 5:00 p.m. came. John Vincent's secretary remained at her desk for another thirty minutes before placing some notes on his desk. As she did so she noticed that he had made a notation about a call from a member of the state's Congressional delegation.

Each day at about sunset a park policeman in a pickup truck drives the entire circuit around the lake on the fire suppression road. A part of his task was to make certain that no one was planning to stay after dark. The picnic grounds were actually on the other side of the lake.

He had started on the far side of the lake so he did not get to John Vincent's car until nearly 7:30 p.m. John's body lay on the other side of the car. He emerged from the pickup and came around the car to find John's body lying face up with the revolver still in his hand. By this time some rigor mortis had set in but he did not try to remove the gun.

Going to his radio he called his headquarters.

"I've found a dead guy around post 57. It looks like he committed suicide. Shall I check for his ID?"

The Park police sergeant at the headquarters had never been trained regarding how to deal with a homicide. In total violation of standard homicide procedures he told the driver of the pickup to go through Vincent's pockets until he found a wallet. When the driver of the pickup found John's wallet he called in his name. He also noted his security credentials from the office of the State Attorney General.

"Just stay put until I call you back. Don't let anyone come around the body until the state police arrive."

The Park headquarters sergeant contacted his superiors. They in turn began the process of contacting the Attorney General's office. By the time that someone had contacted John's wife it was nearly 8:30.

The issue of who should be in charge of the investigation became exacerbated as the Capitol Police and the Capitol City Metropolitan Police arrived at the scene. By this time the Park Police had decided to go through John's car. They had also tramped down much of the foliage around the site which among other things totally obliterated the footprints of Javier when he was taking the photos of John's dead body. This was only the beginning of a series of mistakes made by all of the police officials. They had also obliterated the second set of tire tracks made by the van as well as the footprints around John's car.

When Stuart Livingston was informed he immediately returned to the Capitol. He made contact with Jezebel who could not control her emotions. She told him to locate Willie and to have Willie meet her at John Vincent's home.

Jezebel had returned to John Vincent's office after John's secretary had left for the day. She finally located the file cabinet which contained all of John's files with regard to Jezebel and Willie. When she was confident that she had found them all she left the office to return to Willie's office. A night watchman stationed in the hall offered to help her with the files but she declined. He then noted his watch in case he needed to be certain about the time she left John's office.

Jezebel had been in John's office for nearly an hour while she was searching for the files. By the time she had arrived at their home it was 7:30 p.m. An hour later Stuart Livingston finally contacted her about John's death.

She had carried the files from Vincent's office to her car and then had driven home. When Willie reached her they agreed to meet at the Vincent's home. By this time some extended family had gathered as well as the family's minister from the Presbyterian Church. At this point everyone accepted the Park Policeman's conclusion that John had committed suicide. Willie arrived shortly after Jezebel.

Because of the phone call from the voice Jezebel had been able to reason that John had not taken his own life. However, she joined in the expressions of grief and stunned amazement that he would commit suicide. As soon as it was appropriate Jezebel and Willie left for their own home.

The Capitol Police were no more qualified to deal with the issue of the real cause of John Vincent's death than were the Park Police. By the time that the Capitol City Metropolitan Police were on the scene a number of errors had been made.

Metropolitan Police are trained when investigating a suicide by use of a firearm to look for every possible clue that in fact the decedent had been murdered and the murderer had then staged what appeared to be the decedent's suicide. The worst mistake was that the Park Police had moved John's body so that it was now impossible to re-enact what actually happened at the time of death. The Capitol Police were equally in error by ordering an ambulance to come and pick up the body. When the Metropolitan Police arrived the ambulance was being positioned so that John's body could be placed on the ambulance gurney.

In charge of the Metropolitan Police unit was Detective Lieutenant Scott Masters. Quickly sensing that they had already lost too much extremely important evidence about how John Vincent actually died, Lt. Masters insisted that the body be placed back in the position where the Park Policeman first found it. He also insisted that the gun be returned to John's right hand. However, for whatever reason the Park policeman who had discovered the body had John's right hand holding the gun but not lying on John's chest.

Detective Masters immediately saw the disconnect with the idea that John had committed suicide. The man who killed John in the back of the van had carefully put the gun into John's hand and then holding the gun with John's hand on the trigger had inserted the gun into John's mouth and fired it. The trajectory of the bullet would be up through John's brain and come out the back of his head. A roll of carpeting had been put behind John's head to muffle the sound of the shot and to keep the bullet from ricocheting inside the van. Since no one at the scene knew about the van the fact that there was no blood or brain matter scattered behind where the Park policeman insisted John had been found confirmed that however else John Vincent had died, it had not been while he was sitting on the ground beside his own automobile.

Detective Lt. Masters also soon became aware that his biggest problem in creating an exact scenario of the death scene was the determination of the Park Police and the Capitol Police to make certain that there was nothing in the record that would reflect badly upon themselves.

Thus the Park Police gave inconsistent summaries of what had been done when John Vincent's body was first discovered, by whom and why his automobile was searched, at what exact time did the first call come from the Park Police officer who first discovered the body, who had touched the body, and who had changed the position of the body.

There had been no systematic record kept of the names of those who had come to the scene and at what times. There had been no photographs made of the scene before the body had actually been moved from its original location. The photographs that were taken by the Capitol Police did not have the benefit of flash attachment on the camera and were very dim. The area had not been sealed off so that the condition of the foliage at the time of Vincent's death could be ascertained. A search to find the bullet that killed Vincent would require hundreds of hours because the moving of the body had altered what would have been the trajectory of the bullet.

At the time of his death John had been wearing a suit coat. The coat had been removed by the Capitol Police to determine if there where any other wounds. The coat had been placed in a body bag with other items from John Vincent's automobile. The Capitol Police had called their Medical Examiner and arranged for the first examination of the body to be done at their facility at the Capitol.

Both the Park Police and the Capitol Police were beginning their written reports with the caption "The Suicide of John Vincent." Thus the assumption that John's death was suicide was perpetuated without any corroboration by a qualified person familiar with homicide and suicide.

A group of volunteers wearing traffic control jackets as they gathered trash along the road had come down the road after the Park Police arrived. When they were turned away no one asked their names or determined if at any time they had seen other persons or automobiles near the death site. Thus the possibility of finding witnesses was lost. The same was true when two joggers came along the road and were immediately sent away by the Park Police without trying to identify who they were or what they may have seen.

Most distressing to Masters was the fact that both the Park Police and the Capitol Police had handled the death weapon and had changed the location of John's hand holding the death weapon when he was first discovered.

So many people had been walking through the brush around the death site that all of the possible evidence of determining that Javier and Annabella had been sitting by the lakeside directly opposite to where John's car was located was lost. The same was true of the tire tracks made by the van.

But if Detective Lt. Masters thought he had problems because of the self-serving exculpatory statements by the Park Police and the Capitol Police, it turned out that they were nothing compared to the conflicting demands and inconsistent explanations from the office of the Attorney General. The only issue upon which there was no discrepancy was determining the time that John Vincent left the Attorney General's suite at the Capitol.

Essentially most of the critical information that Masters needed regarding the death site at the time of death had been rendered totally useless by the Park Police and the Capitol Police after they arrived.

Detective Lieutenant Masters was at his desk by 7:00 a.m. the following morning even though he had not arrived at his home until 1:00 a.m. His first priority was to seek out the help of the FBI and their forensic lab specialists regarding the death weapon. The Capitol Police had taken the gun with them when they left the death scene with John's body, his clothing, and his automobile.

Masters' next priority was to interview the personnel at the Attorney General's office. As he was preparing to make that call his immediate superior, the Deputy Chief of the Metropolitan Police came to his office.

"Scott, I understand you had a late night. Thank you for keeping the situation from getting totally out of hand. But I have just gotten off the phone with the Attorney General. He wants to give the exclusive jurisdiction for this matter to the Capitol Police. All you have to do is complete your report and give it to me. I in turn will forward it to the Capitol Police and it will be out of our hands."

Masters began to give an explanation of all that had been done wrong, or worse, had not been done at all during the evening and night at the death site. The Deputy Chief raised his hand to signal to Masters that he could save his breath. "This thing is so fraught with politics that the last thing we want is to have jurisdiction of this case. Be grateful for small blessings."

With that the Deputy Chief arose and said, "Get your report to me as soon as possible." He then left the room.

Masters completed his report and hand delivered it to the office of the Deputy Chief. He had been back at his desk for less than an hour when the secretary to his group buzzed him on the intercom to ask if he was available to take a call from a reporter form the *Capitol Times* by the name of Kathy Christiansen. Like most of his colleagues in law enforcement he had an inherent distrust of the media because irrespective of what you told them they used their interview with you to put their own spin on whatever the subject of the interview might have been.

Other reporters for the *Times* had covered the story of John Vincent's death. By the time the paper had gone to press there were still a huge number of unknown matters. Master's paused for a moment but then decided to take the call since he could now explain that the matter was out of his hands.

"Put it through," he informed the secretary.

Kathy began the conversation with a disclaimer that she was a reporter. "I am not one of the reporters covering this story," she explained. "I am a columnist for the editorial page but would be most grateful if you could help me to understand how the investigation is now proceeding. I will not presume to quote you without your specific permission."

That last comment by Kathy was much more important than she realized. Masters had only planned to tell her of the decision by the Attorney General to have the Capitol Police be the primary entity dealing with the events surrounding the death of John Vincent. With that he intended to terminate the conversation.

"As long as you can confirm that anything I tell you is not for publication I will do whatever I can to help you," he said.

"You have my promise," said Kathy, "unless you specifically approve of anything I write it will remain totally confidential."

Masters then proceeded to inform Kathy of the decision to have the entire matter handled by the Capitol Police and the instructions given to him by the Deputy Chief.

"I cannot ever remember a situation when the Capitol Police were responsible for dealing with the death of a state official," she said. "That seems to be a very peculiar decision. What do they know about homicide investigations?"

Kathy's use of the term 'homicide' was not lost upon Masters. Still, he was very reluctant to comment on the obvious fact that it is far from certain that John Vincent took his own life.

"It appears that the decision has been made that this was a suicide and so the Attorney General wants to keep the investigation under his control," responded Masters.

"Do you agree with that conclusion?" pressed Kathy.

Here Masters determined that he had already said more than it was safe for him to say with a representative of the press.

"My opinion is not at issue," he said, "with that decision our department is no longer involved."

By the tone of his voice Kathy could tell that he in fact did not agree with the decision. It was also apparent that he was not going to tell her anything else without the approval of his superiors.

"I think that I understand what you are saying," responded Kathy. "May I get back to you if I have any other questions?

"No problem," said Masters. "Feel free to call any time."

Kathy had been a journalist for over ten years. Over that period of time she had interviewed hundreds of public officials. She knew exactly what Masters' responses meant and decided that it would be much more likely to get his help if she dealt with the people at the A.G.'s office and waited to get back to Masters until she had more information.

Her next call was to the office of the Attorney General. She was finally directed to Stuart Livingston whose title was "Director of the Office of Personnel Security." Livingston had been the one to go to the morgue and confirm the identity of John Vincent. As a result of that and other issues he had been too busy to read the memo on his desk from Willie to all staff in the office of the A.G. that all inquiries regarding the death of John Vincent should be referred to him.

When he answered the phone Kathy introduced herself and again explained that she was not a reporter for the *Times* but a columnist on the editorial page.

"I understand that the Attorney General has decided to have the Capitol Police carry out the investigation on the death of John Vincent. Can you tell me who the contact person is at their office that I should call?"

Livingston was the quintessential political junkie who hungered for the opportunity to qualify to be in the limelight. He was not about to lose the opportunity to become an important contact for someone with Kathy's credentials at the *Capitol Times*.

"We are conducting the investigation insofar as the office of the Attorney General is concerned," he said. "The Capitol Police are taking care of the specific issues regarding the suicide itself. How can I help you?

Here Kathy had to be very cautious not to intrude into the domain of the staff reporters who were covering the story. She simply said, "Could you tell me what has been determined within your office as to why John Vincent would take his own life?"

Here Livingston went far beyond what was prudent for him to say although neither Web Reno nor Jezebel were there for him to ask for guidance.

"Vincent had been working on a number of critical issues for the state and was obviously fatigued by the load he was carrying. At the moment it appears that he simply determined that it was too much for him to continue to bear that burden."

Kathy now sensed that she had someone who had very little experience in dealing with the media and was presuming to make comments way beyond what he was in fact qualified to say.

"Why was Mr. Vincent out at the lake yesterday? Did he have some appointment there or was it just a way to get to a remote place where he could take his own life?"

Now even Livingston knew that he had passed the line of prudent caution and was over his head. "We are still dealing with that and some other issues. I will just have to get back to you when we have more details confirmed."

"May I get back to you later today?" asked Kathy.

"Probably tomorrow would be better," said Livingston. "Please call me in the morning."

As that conversation ended Web Reno himself came to Livingston's desk and hand delivered a memo for all of the staff that all inquiries from the media should be referred to him only and not to the designated spokesperson for the A.G.

"Get this circulated throughout the office," said Reno. "Willie and I will be holding a staff meeting in the conference room in about an hour. Have your people be there." With that he walked away.

When Willie and Jezebel had arrived back at their home from their meeting with John Vincent's wife it was the first time since the election that Jezebel was not determining what the priorities would be. The phone call from the voice and the confirmation that John Vincent was dead had left her totally incapable of any objective analysis of what needed to be done. Willie gave her a tranquilizer and sent her to bed.

At 11:00 p.m. Willie phoned the designated emergency contact member of the staff with the instructions that no one was to respond to press inquiries or other matters involving John Vincent's death until he personally was at the office in the morning. That instruction was one of several items on Livingston's desk that he had not read.

The next morning when a senior officer of the Capitol Police by the name of Monagan had come to the Attorney General's office he was directed to Livingston. His mission was to set up a time to interview the people in the office who had dealt with John Vincent yesterday. Livingston was relieved to be able to direct him to Web Reno as the contact person for the office of the A.G.

At 11:00 a.m. the conference room used for larger meetings was filled with the personnel who actually work in the personal suite of offices of the Attorney General. Willie was more than capable of dealing with the matter in such a way that evinced both emotion and determination to carry on through the crisis.

"It has been a very difficult night and morning for myself and my wife. We have treasured our association with John Vincent not only as a cousin but as a friend and brother. Our condolences to John's wife and family were expressed to them at their home last night."

Even though the office of the A.G. had a designated spokesperson whose task it was to respond to the media Willie had personally informed him during the late night hours that he was not to make any public comment about John's death until after a meeting with the critical personnel in the morning.

When the Capitol Police officer who had come to Livingston was allowed to talk to Web Reno he was invited by Reno to come into the meeting with Willie and the key staff people.

Willie then instructed the staff that he had instructed Web Reno to be the designated spokesperson for the office and that all inquiries were to be referred to Reno. He then turned the meeting over to Reno.

"The Capitol Police will be contacting some of you who were working closely with John Vincent. Officer Monagan who is here in the room with us will be directing that process. Please give Officer Monagan and those working with him your total cooperation. However, any documents that were a part of John Vincent's responsibility are to be provided to me and not to the Capitol Police officials. I will then determine how to proceed with whether or not to provide the police with copies of those documents."

Reno briefly responded to the obvious questions. By 11:30 the meeting was over and Reno then instructed officer Monagan and John Vincent's secretary to come to his office.

7

"AMONG THE LIVING ARE THE DEAD"

The afternoon after the death of John Vincent, officer Monagan and a second officer from the Capitol Police interviewed John Vincent's secretary, the other personnel who had been present when John left at approximately 1:00 p.m., and the last person in the office to see John Vincent alive, the security guard on duty at the entrance to the Attorney General's suite. When asked a direct question by Officer Monagan about any visitors to John's office the security guard also mentioned that Jezebel, the wife of the Attorney General, had come out of John's office at about 5:30 p.m. with some files.

At the instruction of Webster Reno, none of the papers on John's desk or in his office were to be moved.

The next day the Capitol Police returned John's car to his wife at their residence.

On the third day after John's death the Capitol Police announced that the evidence available conclusively showed that John Vincent had committed suicide. With that announcement the Capitol Police closed their file on the case.

That same afternoon a mail clerk at the *Capitol Times* brought a small package wrapped in brown paper to the office of Edwin Martin. It was Friday afternoon and Martin was getting prepared for his meeting with Orson Goldman and Kathy Christiansen. The death of John Vincent would consume all of the scheduled time for the meeting.

Casually Martin opened the small package to find a disposable camera and a lone piece of paper with what appeared to be a license plate number written on it. Perplexed Martin asked his secretary to have their photo lab develop the film in the camera and let him know if there was something important on the film.

His secretary waited until her afternoon break to take the film to the photo lab. The people there were busy preparing the Saturday and Sunday editions of the paper and asked if it could wait until Monday. Having no reason to say otherwise she simply said, ". . . get them back to me on Monday."

Willie was now well into his third year as the Attorney General. He had managed to bury the controversy over the deaths of Zach and Zeke by getting the federal government to take control of the case. The Special Prosecutor assigned to the case had been hounded and harassed by Reno until she finally resigned and moved out of the state. Kathy Christiansen's exclusive article of the Deputy Prosecutor's story caused a momentary stir but as the months went by the federal investigation simply faded away.

The embarrassing fact that Jezebel's brother Paul was a partner in the law firm that netted over fifty million dollars out of the state's share of the tobacco industry settlement was essentially shrugged off by the citizenry at large.

Even the rumors about Willie's sexual escapades had become so common that most people simply shake their heads and went on with their own business.

As Orson Goldman and Kathy Christiansen sat at Edwin Martin's conference table the announcement by the Capitol Police that their investigation of the death of John Vincent had confirmed that Vincent was a victim of severe depression and overwork would be in the next morning issue of the *Times*. A copy of the Park Police report was delivered to their office.

Kathy sat quietly as Orson and Edwin reviewed the week's events, the announcement by the Capitol Police that John's death was a suicide, and the many expressions of sympathy to John Vincent's family from government officials and other community leaders.

"I feel sorry for Hilton," said Orson. "John Vincent was the strongest attorney in his office. It will take a remarkable person to replace him. He was the key negotiator with regard to both the tobacco industry's settlement and the Canadian's proposal to build a uranium enrichment facility in the state."

Martin then turned to Kathy. "Hilton is more than half-way through his first term as the A.G. Are you ready to cut him some slack or are you still doubtful?" Martin had been a graduate of the U.S. Naval Academy and went on to obtain advanced degrees from Yale and Cambridge University in England. The naval term of "cutting some slack" hearkened back to the days of sailing ships.

Kathy sat silently for a moment. Then without any apology to the two men in the room she said "I not only have not changed my original opinion, but have in fact strengthened it. My guess is that we have not heard the last of the strange death of John Vincent. The use of the Capitol Police to make this investigation made as much sense as inviting a local troop of boy scouts to carry it out. They were determined from the very beginning to get it over with before someone found out that they did not know what they were doing. I have seen nothing about the results of their investigation that gives any substance to the conclusion that John Vincent took his own life."

Goldman could not resist coming back once again to the point he had made so many times about Willie Hilton. "The A.G. has held up like a brick wall. He and Vincent were cousins as well as graduates in the same class at law school. I am told that Vincent was to deliver the annual "Founder's Day" lecture next week for the law school. I hope that they ask Hilton to replace him on the program."

"Well, Kathy," said Martin, "let's get on with the issues that people want to hear about. What do you recommend for next week? Is there anything going in the legislative session that merits special attention?"

For the next hour the three people who had the most influence upon what the politically active people in the state Capitol would think and talk about during the next seven days continued to examine the short list of issues that were important to them. It was finally decided that Goldman would do a "scorecard" on the legislature for the first four months of their legislative session and Kathy would develop some further background about the Canadian company's petition to enter into a contract with the state for a uranium enrichment plant to be located out in the southwestern portion of the state.

As they stood to depart for their weekend activities Martin asked, "Do either of you know why someone would send me a disposable camera? Have we got a contest of some kind going on that I do not know about?"

Both Orson and Kathy shook their heads in the negative and with that they began to mentally relax in anticipation of two days of quiet unwinding.

On Monday morning Edwin Martin attended a town hall meeting by one of the State's two United States Senators. He did not arrive at the office until 10:30 a.m. A few minutes after arriving his secretary buzzed on the intercom to say that the director of the photo lab was at her desk asking to see Martin.

"Send him in," responded Martin.

The director of the photo lab entered with a large envelope in his hand and a serious look in his countenance.

"Good morning Ed. Last Friday you sent a disposable camera down to us and asked that we develop the film."

"Yes, I remember. Is it something important?"

"Take a look."

The director of the photo lab laid out six 8 x 10 color photos. Martin spent several minutes just looking at them and then said, "Has anyone else seen these?"

"Just the two guys in the dark room."

"Please make certain that they say absolutely nothing to anyone about these photos. Absolutely nothing! Is that clear."

With that Martin excused the photo lab director and called Orson Goldman and Kathy Christensen on the intercom. Only Kathy answered.

"Good morning Ed. What's up?"

"Kathy, where is Orson?"

"I'm not sure. I haven't seen him all morning."

"Please come to my office as soon as possible."

Martin had laid out the six photos on the small conference table in his room. As Kathy came in he simply gestured at the photos. When Kathy looked her casual demeanor quickly changed as she gasped "What on earth. . . ." She did not finish the sentence.

Kathy slumped down into a chair and picked up one of the two photos of John Vincent with the camera pointed directly down at his face. There were also two photos taken from each side of his body, and two more photos of his car and the surrounding underbrush.

"Do you know who took them?" she asked.

"I have no idea. I received a small package last week with a disposable camera in it and sent it down to the photo lab for development. He brought these back to me ten minutes ago."

"Was anything else in the package? Did it have a return address?"

"I really don't remember. It seems to me that there was a piece of white paper with something written on it." With that Martin returned to his desk and after a moment came back to the table with the small piece of paper that was in the package.

"Ed. I would like to call Detective Lt. Masters at the Metropolitan police. He was the senior police officer at the scene when John Vincent's body was discovered."

Martin hesitated for a moment but finally said, "Please call him but do not tell him why. Just inform him that we have something very important for him to look at and ask him to come over as quickly as possible."

When Kathy got through to Masters she made certain that he understood that this was not a request based on the question "if you have the time." Masters listened carefully and then simply said, "I will be right over. Where do I meet you?

Masters arrived in less than fifteen minutes. Martin and Kathy said nothing but simple gestured to the photos on the conference table. After Masters had collected his thoughts Martin gave him the same explanation regarding how he obtained the photos as was given to Kathy.

Masters picked up the piece of paper and using his cell phone he called his office. He simply said, "This is a highest priority request. I need to get all of the registration information for this license plate number. Get back to me as soon as possible."

Finally Masters turned to Martin and Kathy. "It is obvious that whoever took these photos did so before the Park Police were on the scene. From the position of shadows in the photos it appears that they were taken in the mid-afternoon, at least two or three hours before the Park Police discovered Vincent's body. I can tell you now with certainty that John Vincent did not kill himself. Had he put the revolver into his mouth and fired it neither his head nor the gun would have ended up in that position."

Masters' cell phone rang. He turned on the speaker so that Kathy and Martin could hear the conversation.

"Scott, the license plate number was for a rented delivery van. It was rented at the airport last Tuesday morning and returned late afternoon. The name and address of the person who rented it is phony which means that they had corrupted ID. That's all I could find out."

"OK" said Masters " Now listen carefully. Get a search warrant as soon as possible. I want that van picked up immediately and taken to the forensic lab. I want it dusted from bumper to bumper. I also want someone to take a search warrant out to the home of John Vincent and get the clothing that he was wearing last Tuesday. I will be back to the office before noon."

"What's going on, Scott."

"I'm holding in my hand a photograph taken of John Vincent after he was killed and before anyone from the Park service got to the scene. In my opinion the photograph proves that there was no way John Vincent killed himself. Please tell the Deputy Chief that this is extremely confidential. I will go over all of the details with him when I get back to the office. Do not let anyone else in the office know what I have told you until I return. Get those evidence warrants immediately."

Masters turned to Martin and Kathy. "I will need to take these with me. Do you want a receipt or can you trust me to get them back to you?"

Martin said, "Of course. When can we break the story?"

"Please give me enough time to go through that van from front to back and top to bottom. I want to find out if that van was how Vincent ended up in the park. I want to know if Vincent's body was carried in the van. I want to start a tracer on the individual who rented the van. By the end of the day I will tell you what I have learned and you can then break the story."

With that Masters gathered up the photos and left the office.

Martin and Kathy sat silently for several minutes. Finally Martin said, "Well Kathy, your intuition of last Friday turns out to be correct. This will be your story. When Goldman returns to the office have him come and see me immediately. After you have spoken to Lieutenant Masters and have your story let me see it before we send it to the press room."

Kathy returned to her office. On her desk was the copy of the "final report" that the Park Service had prepared regarding the "suicide" of John Vincent. She opened the report and started to go through it line by line.

It was 5:30 p.m. when Kathy heard back from Detective Lt. Masters. "I have just returned from a brief meeting with John Vincent's wife. She has had a very difficult week but she seems to be all right at the moment. She has agreed to keep our meeting confidential until I get back to her.

Because of the way in which we obtained these photographs I have been given permission to share with you what we have learned. You can go ahead with your story. We will be holding a press conference tomorrow morning at 10:00 a.m. This is what we have learned so far.

- John Vincent was dead by 2:30 p.m. We have been able to read his wrist watch on one of the photographs.
- He was killed in the van. The rental agency remembered that a piece of new carpeting was still in the van when it was returned. They rescued it from the garbage dumpster when our people picked up the van. Apparently he was unconscious when they killed him. They had rolled the carpet up and put it behind his head and then put the gun in

his mouth and pulled the trigger. The bullet was still in the carpet with blood and skull fragments as well.

- We found threads from the mat on the floor of the van in John Vincent's clothing.
- There was still some soil in the tire treads of the van. We are checking that out to see if it was from the dirt road in the park.
- The murderer or murderers apparently flew into the airport on Tuesday morning and left again Tuesday night. There are no passengers listed for arrival or departure that match the name used to rent the van.
- Our department has re-opened the investigation as a homicide.
- There are no fingerprints in the van or on the outside. The van went through the wash when it was returned.
- We have asked the Park Service to return the revolver but they are resisting our request.

Our assumption is that whoever took those photographs was not involved in the murder but for whatever reason do not want to be identified. We were able to rescue the disposable camera from the photo lab but there were no fingerprints on it. The box and paper in which it came to Mr. Martin's desk went out with the trash last Friday.

Our most urgent priority is to find whoever took the photographs and see if they saw anyone else around the body or John Vincent's car.

That is about all that we have learned. If we find out anything else I will let you know."

Kathy finished writing the story and got it to the press room around 8:30 p.m. After reading Kathy's story Martin had decided not to use one of the photographs in the story. The story would appear in the morning edition of the paper but Martin also decided to put the story on their wire service at 9:00 p.m.

Kathy finished her "take out" dinner at her desk and then prepared to leave. Something Detective Masters had mentioned to her made her stop and go back to the report from the Park Service. On the page where Officer Monagan of the Park Service had questioned Jezebel about the files that she had taken from John Vincent's office she said that she had spoken briefly to John Vincent around 4:00 p.m. That was when he had asked her to get the files.

The watch on John Vincent's wrist that showed in the photograph made it clear that John was already dead by 2:30 p.m.

8

UNDER PENALTY OF DEATH

As soon as Willie had won the election Jezebel arranged to obtain her own private server for her use for e-mail and document transfers. On this particular morning as she opened up her e-mail account she found a four page document that had come during the night from London. The document was a Banker's Draft and Certificate of Deposit that had originated with the Morgan Guaranty Trust Co. and was addressed to Intercontinental Financial Systems, Inc. The document was a draft for five hundred million Euros (E500,000,000.00).

With the document was a "Confirmation Letter" over the names and signatures of the Vice Chairman and Chief Executive Officer of the originating bank. The Confirmation Letter contained all of the data necessary to authenticate the draft including the Registration Number for the International Monetary Fund and the Banker's draft number.

Even as she was examining the documents her cell phone rang. It was the Voice who said, "Several hours ago you received a four page document. Have you opened or printed that document?

"I just started reading my e-mail messages. I opened it because I had no idea where it came from. I have not printed it."

"Listen very carefully to what I am about to tell you. I will give you a six letter and six numeral sequence. Immediately enter that into your computer without saving the document or printing it. Your life could well depend on doing exactly what I tell you. Please do it right now."

Jezebel immediately entered the six letters and the six numerals as requested and the document disappeared.

"OK," she said, "it is gone now." She knew better than to ask any question. After three years of one way conversations with the Voice she had learned that it was much better not to ask.

"What you have just learned is very unfortunate. It makes it necessary to have you come to London as soon as possible. You will get an itinerary for your travel and hotel. All of the expenses will have been pre-paid. You do not need to pack many clothes, you will only be in London for a few days. This is not a request. It is an order and your life depends upon it."

At first Jezebel was quite offended. Then as she began to think things through she realized that if she was shrewd enough while in London it could be the single most important opportunity of her life. As she pondered the last three years she remembered the first one hundred thousand dollars for the cattle futures options; the five hundred thousand dollars for the Bluewater project; the decision by the federal officials not to continue the investigation into the deaths of Zeke and Zach; the enormous benefits that had come from dealing with the Japanese and the Canadians regarding the Uranium deposit and possible ore concentrating and refining facility; the death of John Vincent when it became certain from his personal journals that he was going to inform someone of what had been going on in the State Attorney General's Office; and now a transfer of a sum of such great wealth that she needed a calculator to determine what it was in dollars.

"How soon will the travel details come?" she said.

"In less than two hours. You will be leaving by late afternoon your time. Make certain that you are on that plane."

Without waiting for the travel memo to come she informed Willie that she would be out of town for a few days. When he asked where she was going she simply said, "to the airport." Since Willie could care less where she went or why he simply changed the subject and shortly thereafter left for the state Capitol building. Jezebel flew to New York where she boarded a Delta flight to London.

The next morning she landed at London's Heathrow Airport. As she exited the airport security area a man held up a contact sign with her name on it. She had no other luggage than her carry-on. He led her to a limousine and after an hour of fighting the London traffic she was at one of the most exclusive and posh hotels in London.

After checking in she was informed that arrangements had been made for her to receive the most comprehensive beauty spa treatments that money could buy. After five hours of every conceivable beauty enhancing application available she returned to her room. There was a message on her phone from the Voice that there would be a dinner meeting at 7:00 p.m. He suggested that she take a nap because it was likely to be a long meeting.

Just before 7:00 p.m. there was a knock on her door. The driver of the limo that brought her from the airport offered to escort her to the meeting room. There she was introduced to three other individuals, two men and a woman. Not one of whom was the "Voice."

After introductions as dinner was served the conversation was animated but not presumptuous. The topics discussed turned to the current international issues as well as the banal subject of world famous individuals and personalities. Finally after dessert and a glass of the $1,200.00-per-bottle liquor that was provided to each person present the evident host for the evening turned the conversation to the serious issues with which the group were concerned.

The individual who spoke was both intimidating and yet non-threatening. He was the quintessential example of the European aristocratic courtier.

"We have been very interested in watching the career of your husband since we first met you in New York with the Chairman of the Springville Foundation," he said. "Very frankly, we probably would not have remained so interested in his career if it had not been for the very impressive way that you presented yourself on that occasion. Since then it has been your skillful handling of his political career that has kept us willing to continue to support you."

If there was one gift that Jezebel had nurtured for many years it was the ability to appear to be a good listener. This time she was not feigning the interest. Every cell in her brain was focused at maximum power in order that she would not miss the meaning or the purpose of what she was being told.

"It was most unfortunate that the document you received was transmitted to you by mistake. However, in this instance the mistake has turned out to be positive in that it forced us to determine what our future course of action with you would be. We have also had serious concern regarding some of your husband's bizarre conduct."

Without saying so, he was referring—among other things— to Willie's rape of Juanita Fields, of which Jezebel as yet had no knowledge. One of Willie's security detail had been all too willing to receive extra compensation for his detailed reports of Willie's conduct and conversations.

The courtier continued, "Your skill in dealing with the delegation from Japan and our mutual friend from Canada was very encouraging to us."

As he was speaking Jezebel's mind was running at full speed down three separate tracks. When he referred to "we" just who or what was he talking about? What did they have in common with Arnold Tucker, the Canadian billionaire who wanted an exclusive right to exploit the uranium deposits? And exactly what is their ultimate objective and how do I (Jezebel) fit into their strategy? By the end of the next two hours Jezebel had the answers to all three questions.

"We are inviting you to become an inside participant with our international financial combination," he continued. "That means that we are committed to doing all in our power (which he might have added was overwhelming) to see your husband reach his potential in the world of American politics. There is only one prerequisite that you must meet in order to confirm your acceptance of this invitation. That prerequisite is an absolute and unqualified covenant of loyalty to and confidentiality regarding our existence and our objectives."

At this point the courtier stopped and stared intently into Jezebel's face. When Jezebel realized that he was waiting for her to affirm her willingness to become associated with them under the terms and conditions he had described she smiled, and with all of the conviction that she could feign she said, "I am overwhelmed that you would consider me worthy of such an honor. By all means you have my total and complete acceptance of your proposal and of the terms and conditions that you have set."

At that point the courtier and both of his associates expressed their delight with Jezebel's response. She in turn felt an immense sense of relief that she was not dreaming but in reality had just been made a member of their secret combination. What she did not understand was that her response also saved her life. She would never have left the hotel alive had it been otherwise.

The other two participants in the meeting then gave some brief explanation of how they would fit into Jezebel's future. From time to time Jezebel would meet them in various contexts as the wife of Willie Hilton. They were to be treated by Jezebel no differently than others who for whatever reason would be involved with any specific endeavor, political or business.

"There is one important bit of information that you will want to take home with you," said the courtier. "The Governor has definitely decided that he will not seek a third term. We would like Willie to prepare to announce that he will be a candidate for Governor. As happened with your campaign of three years ago, all of the financial support that you will need will be provided. We want you to continue with your present participation in his political life."

There followed another several hours of conversation about the Governor's race and the strategy that would be needed to win the nomination and the election. Finally just after midnight Jezebel was escorted back to her room. As she was leaving the Courtier presented her with a velvet jewel case which contained a necklace, earrings, a bracelet, and a brooch. They had been purchased that day for just over fifty thousand dollars at Tiffany's in London.

Jezebel was effusive in her expression of gratitude. The female member of the delegation then said, "I would love to take you shopping tomorrow before your flight. I think we can find some things that you will enjoy." So it was arranged that she would come to Jezebel's room at 10:00 a.m. Her flight to New York would depart at 5:00 p.m. from Heathrow. Her connection back to the State Capitol from New York would be at 4:00 p.m. Eastern Time.

The shopping trip was an experience in superlatives. While they were shopping the female member of the delegation explained to Jezebel that she was the wife of an international business executive who divided his time between Europe and the United States east coast. She told Jezebel that at some time soon she and her husband would invite them to be their guests at an exclusive resort in the Bahamas. She also said that she and Jezebel would no doubt be meeting each other frequently in Washington, D.C. and other major American cities once Willie was elected Governor.

She also told Jezebel that in addition to telling Willie that he was going to run for Governor one of Jezebel's assignments after she had returned home was to create a non-profit foundation with the mission to engage in various charitable endeavors in other countries. As part of her initiation into the world of multibillion dollar machinations it was explained to Jezebel that having a foundation to which individuals in foreign countries could make unlimited contributions would be of enormous benefit to a Governor who needed to find a way for foreigners to provide substantial financial support without any interference by the state or federal election code.

Within a few weeks the Willie and Jezebel Hilton Charitable-Education Foundation was filed with the State Corporations Commission as a non-profit charity. An application to the Internal Revenue Service to classify the foundation as a 501 c 3 tax exempt entity was also filed.

Jezebel did not even think of sleep as she lounged in her first class seat on the flight to New York. Her mind was aflame with the realization that she was now part of an entity that possessed more wealth and power than she had ever conceived existed. And in her mind was the image that had appeared on her computer monitor three days before and the figure of five hundred million Euros.

Upon her arrival home Jezebel finds that Willie is in serious political trouble. During the past several months an investigator for the State Senate Committee on Government Operations had become curious about Stuart Livingston's increasingly luxurious life style in the three years since Willie took office.

An investigation into the underwriting contracts that had been awarded to Lamberger's company included a subpoena of all of the documentation surrounding these contracts. Lamberger's attorneys stonewalled the subpoena for as long as possible. When that documentation is finally provided the "kickbacks" from Lamberger to Webster Reno and Stuart Livingston finally come to light.

Criminal indictments were issued against both Reno and Livingston. On the eve of the day that the trial was to begin both men offer to "plea bargain" with the prosecutors. Jezebel met privately with Livingston and assures him that if he keeps his mouth shut about her "gifts" from the Japanese she will make certain that at the right time the Governor commutes his sentence. Livingston decides that trusting her commitment is a better way to keep some future for himself with Willie and Jezebel than anything that the prosecutors could offer him.

Both Reno and Livingston resign from their positions. Reno pleads guilty to two fraud felonies in a deal with the Prosecutors in which he promised future cooperation. No cooperation was ever forthcoming.

The court gives them each thirty month sentences. Ultimately neither of them serve more than eleven months in prison.

Shortly after most people have forgotten about John Vincent, Zach and Zeke and Reno and Livingston, Willie announces that he will run for Governor.

9

EPILOGUE

One unanticipated result of Kathy's reading of her journals from the past four years was a decision to accept the invitation from New York. Willie was going to be elected as governor. Jezebel would be there as always skillfully defiantly defending her corrupt and venal husband. Willie and Jezebel had succeeded in turning the office of the Attorney General into an elaborate criminal enterprise. Just think of what they could do if the entire state was under their control from the Governor's office.

Kathy found a note that she had written when Jezebel was explaining the fact that she was asking people to believe that by studying *The Wall Street Journal* she was able to make a 10,000 percent profit in her commodity trading and use the money in her husband's first campaign for Attorney General. After listening to Jezebel tell her story Kathy's note was **". . . of course she had to tell the lie because it was necessary to keep her from admitting that she had essentially taken a one hundred thousand dollar bribe."**

Then there was the scandal that arose when it was revealed that Stuart Livingston had used his position as head of the Attorney General's Office of Personnel Security to create a data base of the names of over twenty thousand people in the state by using the Attorney General's authority to access their state income tax returns. She had denied any knowledge of what Livingston was doing until Paula Corbin Smith, one of the female employees whom Willie had pressured to engage in sex with him, released some documents showing that Jezebel was constantly using that data base for fund raising purposes on behalf of their foundation.

The female employee had resigned when another female employee by the name of Jennifer Rose was more accepting of Willie's advances and was given the position in the office that had been promised to her.

Kathy then turned to her journal entries surrounding the murder of John Vincent. The murder was never solved and though the Metropolitan Police Department's file on the murder was still open the individual who had taken the photographs of John Vincent's body had never come forward.

At first Jezebel had denied taking any files from John Vincent's office. Her lie was countered by the Security Guard employed by the Capitol Police. Even then she publicly defended her lie claiming that it was necessary because of her concern for Vincent's wife and children. She also defiantly supported Willie's refusal to allow the Metropolitan Police to have access to Vincent's files or the papers on his desk.

Though Kathy did not know it, had the Metropolitan Police been allowed to do so they would have found John Vincent's hand written note about the phone call from a member of Congress on the day he was murdered. It was that phone call that had taken him to the small restaurant by the lake and his murderer.

Kathy then had written in her journal the comment by Detective Lt. Scott Masters that he considered **Jezebel's conduct as "obstruction of justice" a felony for which she should have been prosecuted.**

Then she turned to the bizarre episode of how Webster Reno and Stuart Livingston had taken "kickbacks" from Dan Lamberger when he was awarded several state contracts for underwriting bonds on state projects that were contracted by the State with third party providers.

At the insistence of the leaders of the State legislature an independent counsel was retained by the state to investigate the entire matter. During the investigation into Lamberger's kickbacks to Reno and Livingston Jezebel had given sworn testimony that she had not been involved in the decisions to give those contracts to Lamberger. When later evidence given by Lamberger in an attempt to keep himself out of jail proved that she had in fact promised him these contracts the Independent Counsel cited her for perjury because it had resulted in "**a substantial interference with the administration of justice.**"

The decision to pursue this charge against Jezebel was dropped when she simply accused Lamberger of lying to save his own skin. The independent prosecutor could not find any evidence to confirm Lamberger's charges. It was Jezebel's word against a man who was a bail bond broker and who was about to go to jail for criminal fraud.

Then Kathy turned to her notes regarding the Bluewater scandal. Jezebel denied that as a stakeholder in the Bluewater

Limited Partnership that she had participated in any of the decisions regarding the use of the funds received from purchasers of the lots owned by Franklin Savings and Loan. Both Jim McFarlane and his wife had to serve jail terms for contempt of court because of their refusal to testify that Jezebel had been involved in any of these decisions.

Of course, neither Kathy nor the Special Prosecutor were aware that the McFarlane's were promised by the Voice that their time in prison would be brief.

As Kathy had gone through her journals she noted for the first time how frequently a matter in the State was ultimately dealt with to the benefit of Willie and Jezebel by someone from Washington. Whether it was the federal courts or the U.S. Department of Justice or even the White House itself what should have been solely a state matter was given sufficient credence that it justified federal pre-emption of the investigation and prosecution of the matter. The federal pre-emption inevitably resulted in the matter being dropped after months and months of stonewalling.

Kathy had become a close friend of Juanita Fields. When Juanita had shared with Kathy the details of being raped by Willie, she had extracted from Kathy an absolute commitment to never repeat what Juanita had told her. Kathy was true to her oath to Juanita that she would never disclose what she had been told. But now as Kathy pulled together the frequent assertions of otherwise responsible individuals about Willie's sexual molestation, she wondered why had Jezebel always joined Willie in condemning the assertion and the asserter as a liar.

"It is one thing for a wife to be willing to be loyal to her husband even when his guilt was so evident" wrote Kathy, but Jezebel was often the source of the maligning of the accuser as being both a hypocrite and a proven liar. "Why is it," she asked herself, "when there have been so many instances of his total lack of fidelity or loyalty in their marriage she continued to be the innocent self-sacrificing wife?"

This woman is just not that kind of person," wrote Kathy. "What is her motive, her incentive, to continue to live with his shamelessness?"

Kathy pondered for a moment over her use of the word *shameless*. "Is it just that they have no capacity to experience shame?" she asked herself. Juanita Fields had told Kathy that on one occasion at a reception for a retired state Supreme Court judge Willie and Jezebel were there and actually came to Juanita and her husband to greet them. Kathy asked herself, "How could anyone be that crass, that insensitive, that evil?"

Yet that is exactly what they were. Willie and Jezebel as human beings were like dumb animals, totally without any capacity to experience or express shame.

Several months earlier the *Capitol Times* had commissioned an in depth survey of people in the state regarding where they obtained their information about specific issues. The results were shocking to the publishers and editors of the *Times*. What the state-wide survey confirmed was how little influence the *Times* had on the body politic as a whole. A maximum of 20% of the people in the state got their news from the *Times* or their local daily newspaper. Fifty-two percent of the people in the state never read about current events. They got their information about current events from television news casts. The other twenty-eight percent got their information from online services and radio.

The overwhelming majority of the people in the state were able to watch Willie and Jezebel on camera deny the facts, not just the allegations, but the facts about their perversions and they would be believed.

As an example, in connection with the Bluewater debacle and Franklin Savings and Loan the Federal Deposit Insurance Corporation's Inspector General concluded that, in order to "**deceive**" federal regulators Jezebel had drafted a real estate document in connection with a sham real estate transaction that later cost taxpayers $4 million in the bailout of Franklin Savings and Loan.

Among the TV networks only CNN aired a report about the Inspector General's finding. No one else knew about it because none of the other TV channels that most people watched carried the story.

Kathy proceeded with her article. "Recently," she wrote, "I gave a speech on a college campus in which I detailed Jezebel Hilton's method of lying: it is bald deceit sold with a wink-and-nod as the price of advancing a progressive agenda in this bigoted country of ours. Many in the audience criticized my insensitivity in publicly referring to the wife of a major government official in such blatant terms.

None of my critics in the audience were able to rebut the point that Mrs. Hilton is a habitual liar who treats truthfulness in politics the way a calorie-counting diner might treat the rum flavored desert as a health tonic. In other words, she will say, do, and be whatever it takes to get her husband elected."

Kathy wrote, "I keep waiting for someone else to note the inherent hypocrisy with someone who speaks so eloquently about inequality in our society as she builds up her personal bank account with trades in futures options that gives her a ten thousand percent return on her investment. She is floating the 'war on women' theme as her foundation takes donations from countries that whip rape victims. She calls for lower college tuition while charging these institutions thousands of dollars for her lectures.

"Her hypocrisy and her inconsistencies are best exemplified in the amendment to the state election code that she requested a member of the state legislature to introduce. Among other things it called for an automatic voter registration at age 18, a 20-day early-voting period and a maximum 30-minute wait period to vote. She also endorsed the idea of a federal law permitting convicted felons to vote and allowing individuals, such as students, who reside in one state to vote in another state.

"Do the people of the state really want a vindictive, wily, self-centered woman who is capable of skillful deceptions as the 'first lady' of the state?" wrote Kathy.

She closed her article with this question to the reader. "How do you explain why the legislature of the state, the printed and electronic media and the courts have never held Willie and Jezebel Hilton accountable for having turned the office of the Attorney General into a vast criminal enterprise? I have tried to find an answer to this question for nearly four years. The only thing that I have been able to come up with is that **somewhere out there is someone, or something, vastly more powerful than the legislature, the courts, and the media that is determined to protect them from the just consequences of their lies, their illegal conduct, and their wanton acts of dishonesty that have led to half a dozen murders.**"

When Kathy had finished the article with citations to various documents that are in the public domain she printed it off and wrote a short memo to her boss. In her memo conveying her article she also included her resignation as an employee and as a member of the editorial board of the paper.

It was now late in the afternoon. So intense had been her concentration that she had not even taken time for lunch. Then for the first time since her mid-morning observation that the day was one of perfect football weather she looked out the window.

The sky was totally overcast with darkness, and a heavy rain had begun to fall.

As she drove out of the garage and headed home she wondered what it would be like to live and work in New York City.

JOHN L. HARMER

BIBLIOGRAPHY

1. PRIVATE JOURNALS OF KATHY CHRISTIANSEN

2. *CLINTON CASH* by Peter Schweizer Harper Collins Publishers 2015

3. *THE STRANGE DEATH OF VINCENT FOSTER, An Investigation,* Christopher Ruddy; The Free Press; A Division of Simon and Schuster, Inc., 1997

4. *TRUST BETRAYED,* Scott Taylor; Regnery Publishing, 2015

5. *Wall Street Journal,* 27 June, 1997 *Tobacco Lawyers: $50 million Men,* Potomac Watch, by Paul A. Gigot

6. *The Washington Times,* 16 May, 1996 *Of Dinner Parties, Justices and God;* by Suzanne Fields, Op Ed.

7. *The Washington Times,* 16 May, 1996 *Bill Clinton's Lost bimbo,* by Eric Felton. (The DailyJournal of "Sweet Connie Hinzey")

8. *The New York Times, March 1992;* The Whitewater Story, by Jeff Gerth

9. *The Wall Street Journal,* 22 February 1999, Editorial, *Juanita's Story,* The Rape of Juanita Broadrick

10. *Schroeder's List;* Robert Potts Research, Inc. Alexandria, Virginia; *Clinton Officials and Friends in jail, in court, in trouble* Fall 1996

11. *The New York Post;* "Clinton Scandals Are Picking Up Steam" by John Crudele 27 May 1997

12. *The Wall Street Journal,* 16 February 1999, page A 23, Global View by George Melloan, *Ruminations About A Recent Event In Washington*

13. *The Washington Times, 08 August, 1996, Editorial: Mrs. Clinton's Stories*

14. *The Washington Times*, 29 September, 1996, *Questions of Character and Leadership,* by William Triplett II, Former Chief Republican Counsel to the Senate Foreign Relations Committee.

15. *The Wall Street Journal,* 12 February 1998, *Obstruction and Abuse: A Pattern:*

    a. The Train Deaths, 1987: "Arkansas State Medical Examiner . . . rules the deaths of teenagers Kevin Ives and Don Henry, found run over by a train, *'accidental,'* saying the boys had smoked too much marijuana and fallen asleep on the tracks. *A second autopsy and grand jury probe, finding evidence of knife wounds and beatings, declared it a homicide. . . .*

    b. 1984: *The Lasater Case:* Governor Clinton's brother, Roger, is arrested for cocaine possession while working at menial jobs for Little Rock 'bond daddy' Dan Lasater, a major Clinton Supporter.

    c. 1985: *Lassater's company is awarded a $30 million state bond underwriting contract.*

    d. *1990:* After serving part of a 30 month sentence on federal charges of drug distribution Lasater is given a State Pardon by Governor Clinton.

    e. *October 1978: Mrs. Clinton begins a series of commodities trades under the guidance of Tyson Foods executive Jim Tyson earning nearly $100,000.00 on an investment of $1,000.00 in highly risky cattle futures.*

    f. *Whitewater:* May 1990: Madison Guaranty S&L owner Jim McDougal is acquitted of bank fraud in Little Rock. November, Gov. Clinton is elected to a second four year term on the promise that he will serve the full term and not seek the Presidency in 1992. March 1992: New York Times reporter Jeff Gerth discloses the Clinton's dealings with Madison Guaranty and the Whitewater land deal. Privately attacking Gerth the Clinton campaign publicly releases a report by Denver lawyer James Lyon clearing the Clintons of improprieties and saying they lost $68,000 on the investment. The issue fades from the campaign. August 31: The Resolution Trust Corp. prepares a criminal referral for the Justice Department alleging possible crimes by Jim and Susan McDougal, and naming the Clintons and Arkansas Lt. Gov. Jim Guy Tucker as possible beneficiaries. May 28: Before an Arkansas jury, Independent Counsel Kenneth Starr wins conviction of Gov. Tucker and Jim and Susan McDougal for bank fraud and conspiracy relating to Madison S&L.

g. *White House Travel Office and the FBI files.* June 5, 1996. After a lengthy stonewall, the White House releases 1,000 of 3,000 documents sought by the House Oversight Committee in the Travel Office affair. Among the documents area requests by White House Personnel Security Chief Craig Livingstone for FBI files on Travel Office head Billy Dale—dated seven months after his dismissal—as well as hundreds of others, including prominent Republicans.

h. *December 6.* 1994, Webster Hubbell pleads guilty to two fraud felonies in a deal with Whitewater prosecutors and promises cooperation. No cooperation materializes.

i. *The Lewinsky Affair:* December 19, 1997. Former White House Intern Monica Lewinsky is served a subpoena in the Paula Jones sexual harassment case against Bill Clinton. January 12, 1998, Linda Tripp, a friend of Lewinsky, contacts Independent Counsel Kenneth Starr with tapes of conversations between the two, in which Lewinsky said she had an affair with the President and intended to lie in her affidavit.

16. Newsweek (Online) *Diary of a Scandal,* January 21, 1998, by Michael Isikoff. "Tripp. . . told Starr's assistants that she had been urged by her lawyers—whom the White House arranged to represent her—not to volunteer information she had about Hillary Clinton's role in Travelgate."

17. *The New York Post,* June 27, 1997, by John Crudele. "Hillary Clinton has left herself (and tax-return co-signer Bill Clinton) open to prosecution for fraudulent loans and the cover-up that followed. As recently as two weeks ago, Starr's office was also asking questions about Hillary Clinton's actions on the night in 1993 White House aide Vincent Foster committed suicide. . . If Starr can prove Hillary Clinton took Foster documents, she will be indicted for Obstruction of Justice. . . "

18. *The Wall Street Journal,* Friday, 18 December, 1998, page A 14, Editorial entitled The Rule of Law. "The investigator probing Madison Savings and Loan, the Whitewater S&L, was yanked off the case and testified that she had experienced a 'concerted effort to obstruct, hamper and manipulate' her work. Justice investigators were refused access to Vincent Foster's office after his suicide. The tax return Mr. Foster prepared for the Clintons did not list as income Jim McDougal's assumption of the Clinton share of the Whitewater debts. Travel Office Chief Billy Dale was prosecuted by Justice but quickly acquitted by a D.D. jury."

JEZEBEL, WILLIE, AND THE VOICE